This was going to be a short flight to Houston, so I didn't have time to get any work done. Even if I did have time, I wouldn't have been able to focus.

My little plan to put on my game face had backfired. My smile had won over a lot of clients and I knew it.

But this time I wasn't sure who had been won over.

The pilot, Luke Worthington, had smelled so subtly masculine. No cologne. Just soap and maybe shampoo. And maybe he had the faint scent of jet fuel about him, mixed in there somewhere. When had I started finding jet fuel sexy?

He'd been wearing dark glasses, so I hadn't been able to see his eyes. Yet I *felt* him looking at me. It was a little disconcerting to know I was being studied and not being able to see his eyes.

His lips had been so close to mine, they had almost connected of their own accord, pulled together like two magnets.

BILLIONAIRE'S UNEXPECTED LANDING

ALSO BY KATHRYN KALEIGH

THE WORTHINGTONS

Second Chance Kisses

Second Chance Secrets

First Time Charm

Three Broken Rules

Second Chance Destiny

Unexpected Vows

Billionaire's Unexpected Landing

Billionaire's Accidental Girlfriend

Begin Again

Love Again

Falling Again

Just Stay

Just Chance

Just Believe

Just Us

Just Once

Just Happened

Just Maybe

Just Pretend

Just Because

BILLIONAIRE'S UNEXPECTED LANDING

THE WORTHINGTONS

KATHRYN KALEIGH

BILLIONAIRE'S UNEXPECTED LANDING

BILLIONAIRE'S ACCIDENTAL GIRLFRIEND PREVIEW

Copyright © 2022 by Kathryn Kaleigh

All rights reserved.

Written by Kathryn Kaleigh.

Published by KST Publishing, Inc., 2022

Cover by Skyhouse24Media

www.kathrynkaleigh.com

No part of this book may be reproduced in any form or by any electronic or mechanical means, including information storage and retrieval systems, without written permission from the author, except for the use of brief quotations in a book review.

This is a work of fiction. Any names, characters, places, or incidents are products of the author's imagination and used in a fictitious manner. Any resemblance to actual people, places, of events is purely coincidental or fictionalized.

To learn more about Kathryn Kaleigh, visit

www.kathrynkaleigh.com

Kathryn Kaleigh

1

SARAH LAWRENCE

I didn't wear the air pods for music. I wore them to keep out the noise from the jet. I had a good first-class seat and no one bothered me, but I needed the quiet to work.

Absently taking a sip of chilled, bottled water, I changed another word on one of my PowerPoint slides. Just one word. Intrinsic to innate.

I was fiddling with it too much. I needed to leave it alone.

But I was nervous. I was a contender for a promotion. It was down to me and one other pharmaceutical representative. A guy by the name of Tyler Lexton.

I'd never even met the guy, but in my mind, he had the advantage because he already lived in Houston and the company we both worked for was based out of Houston.

I had, however, looked him up. He had two years more experience than I did. Another advantage on his side.

I took a deep breath and glanced out the window.

We were descending already.

I checked my watch. Then my electronic ticket.

Something was wrong.

I closed my Macbook Pro and slid it into my leather computer bag.

We were still at least an hour out of Houston. This wasn't my usual route—most of my flights had been in the western region of the country, but I had flown enough to know when a plane was going in for a landing.

I looked for a flight attendant, but, of course, no one was around.

Then the pilot came over the speaker.

"Due to a mechanical issue, we are making an unexpected landing at the airport in the fine city of Abilene, Texas. Don't worry, though, folks, it's not serious. It's just a precaution. We'll have you back in the air in no time at all."

I leaned back in my seat, straightening my black pencil skirt.

I'd been flying at least once a week for years. It had taken me one year after I'd graduated college and taken my first job as a drug representative to get promoted to a territory sales position. I'd gone from regional to territory just that quick.

The next step up was divisional sales manager, but those positions were competitive.

This *precaution* was going to make me late. My presentation wasn't until morning, but if I missed dinner tonight, I would never recover from the disadvantage.

The company, Clinical Pharm Distributing, was hosting a cocktail dinner with the executives and us two contenders. Me and Tyler.

Since I had Wi-Fi, I sent my supervisor a text. Zachary was a successful man who could have moved up the corporate ladder even more, but he had a family in Los Angeles. He and his husband had adopted a little girl. And the next step up would have put him relocating in Houston.

ME: *There is a problem. My plane is landing in Abilene.*
ZACHARY: *Why?*

ME: *A mechanical... precaution.*

ZACHARY: *You'll be late.*

It didn't bother me that Zachary wasn't worried about the problem with the airplane. He was no nonsense. He'd sent me here for an interview and he expected me to be there. On time.

ME: *Nothing I can do.*

ZACHARY: *Hold on. Let me check on something.*

ME: *Not going anywhere.*

I watched as the plane landed on a little runway in what looked like the middle of absolutely nowhere.

Zachary texted back as we taxied down the runway.

ZACHARY: *There are no more flights out of Abilene today. At least none that will get you to Houston.*

This was it. I was going to lose my one time opportunity for a position that rarely came open. No telling how long I would have to wait for an opportunity like this to come open again.

ZACHARY: *Don't worry. I've gotten it taken care of.*

Seriously? Nobody had that much influence over the airlines. Not even Zachary.

2

LUKE WORTHINGTON

*S*o much for my plans for the evening.

It was a beautiful October day and the evening promised to be just as beautiful. Already I could see the full moon high in the sky. The moon on one side of me and the sun on the other. There was no job in the world with a better view. Wouldn't trade it for anything.

Just when I was preparing to fly back to Houston from a drop off in Fort Worth, I got a call from Father. My father, Quinn Worthington, ran Skye Travels. Skye Travels, established by my grandfather Noah Worthington, was one of the biggest private airlines in the country.

I'd always known I would be a pilot and I'd always known I would fly for Skye Travels. But my father ran the company with an iron fist. The funny thing about Father was that he wasn't even a pilot. Grandpa was and he still flew on occasion. They didn't make them like him anymore.

Quinn didn't make the schedule, but when he said the schedule needed to be changed, it got changed. No questions asked.

A flight from L.A. had made an unexpected landing, so I

was making a detour through Abilene, Texas. I'd been there once. Maybe. I'd flown to so many little airports, only a few of them were memorable. Most of them just ran together.

Father had already submitted my travel plan, so all I had to do was to go through the preflight checklist.

I didn't mind. Not really. But I'd planned to have dinner with my cousin, Daniel and his girlfriend. They were driving through and would only be here the one night. We'd planned on having dinner. Looks like dinner was going to be pushed back a bit.

I'd offered a million times to fly him wherever he wanted to go, but my cousin insisted on driving.

Personally I saw no reason to drive when I could fly. It was so much faster and so much more relaxing. No dodging traffic up here in the sky.

I dreaded the day when that changed and the sky was clogged with traffic. It was coming. Maybe not in my lifetime, but some day.

I taxied out onto the runway and waited my turn to take off.

I knew the Fort Worth airport like the back of my hand. This one and the Houston airport where Skye Travels was based.

Thirty minutes later I was in the air headed to Abilene. A short flight to pick up one passenger. I checked my notes. Sarah Lawrence.

I didn't recognize the name.

I had a few people that asked for me and I flew them frequently. Then there were others, like this one, that were just one time customers. They either had some kind of emergency or they were splurging for a special occasion.

The latter were always fun. The former not so much.

Father hadn't given me any additional information about Sarah. No special requests from her. So I entertained myself by filling in the gaps.

It was a short flight on short notice. I'd bet money that she was one of the emergency passengers.

As the wheels touched down at the Abilene airport, I put on my pilot's cap—standard uniform for Skye Travels—and prepared myself to pick up a distraught female. Probably an older woman, if I had to guess. Probably had an adult child in Houston, a professional who had sent for her. Maybe they were having a baby and wanted Granny there.

After a smooth landing, if I did have to say so myself, I taxied over to the private terminal and came to a stop.

A woman wearing a solid black pencil skirt that looked like she'd been melted and poured into, stepped out and started walking toward me. In most definite high heels that gave her a seductive walk that I doubted she was doing on purpose.

Well. If this was my passenger, she was most definitely not someone's granny.

3

SARAH

*F*ollowing Zachary's instructions, I looked for a small jet with Skye Travels splashed across the tail. In red, no less.

Since there were no other planes landing or taking off, it wasn't hard to spot.

Apparently Zachary knew someone who knew someone who owned this airline, Skye Travels. Personally I had never heard of it, but I always flew commercial. First class, when it was available, but commercial nonetheless.

I was probably supposed to wait for him to land and come to me, but I didn't have time for formalities. I was already an hour behind schedule. I would still make it on time, but there would be less time for me to get to the hotel and back to the restaurant.

Worst case scenario, I would have to skip going to the hotel and wear my skirt suit to dinner. That was lesson number one in pharmaceutical sales. Always wear something professional. Always. Always.

I stood outside the plane and looked up at the pilot.

Wearing dark sunglasses, he was looking in my direction, seemingly in no hurry at all.

I crossed my arms. I know he saw me. I was the only person standing on the tarmac.

This man was very likely going to cost me a promotion.

It didn't matter that he didn't create the situation. He was creating it now.

He tipped his pilot's cap.

Seriously? I was most definitely not in California anymore. I'd not spent any time in the rural towns of Texas, but I'd always thought the movies got it wrong. Surely. But nope. They did not.

The man turned his attention away from me to do who knows what.

Not only was he making me late, but the longer I stood here in these heels, the more my feet hurt.

No matter how long I did what I did, I had yet to figure out how to wear high heels without getting sore feet by the end of the day. And I'd tried every brand of shoes I could find. My current shoes had red bottoms that I had purposely chosen for fashion, not for comfort.

And on top of that, the sun was beating down on my head. Thank God it was October, so it wasn't unbearably hot, but I had just gotten my hair highlighted for the interview.

There was nothing good coming out of this.

Then, finally, he got up and lowered the stairs.

"Are you Sarah Lawrence?" he asked.

I didn't say anything. I just started up the stairs.

When I reached the top, he blocked my path and he wasn't moving.

He was standing above me, but I could tell he was a tall, lean, well-built man. About my age, from what I could see.

I put him at about thirty-two. I ignored his charming smile and his sky blue eyes. I also ignored the five o'clock shadow that most women considered swoon worthy and I was not immune. But I was not in the swoony mood at the moment.

"I'M LUKE WORTHINGTON," he said, holding out a hand.

"I'm late," I said, keeping one hand on the rail and the other on my leather bag. "Can you please get me to Houston?"

"Sure thing," he said, finally backing away.

I stepped inside the cabin and sat down, giving my feet immediate relief.

Luke was just standing there, watching me.

I lifted my shoulders, questioningly.

"Do you have luggage?" he asked.

Damn.

"Yes." I looked out the window. In my hurry to get going, I had completely forgotten about my luggage. It always just followed me wherever I went. All the horror stories of lost luggage didn't apply to me. I'd never lost anything.

"Don't worry," he said. "I'll find it."

Then he stepped off the plane and strode toward the terminal.

I leaned back against the seat. What was it with these pilots and their nonchalant attitudes?

First there had been an unexpected landing for a precaution that I wasn't to worry about. Now there was the matter of my luggage that I also was not to worry about.

I blew out a breath.

I could not blame Luke for this. I should have realized I didn't have my luggage and not just assumed it would follow along with me. I could have tracked it down while I waited for him.

I tapped my fingers against my phone. I mentally rerouted my evening. I would just skip the hotel and go straight to the restaurant.

Stretching my hands out in front of me, I took some deep breaths.

I would grab an Uber or a taxi, whatever was available and go straight to the restaurant. I could pay the driver to take my luggage to the hotel. I'd done that before with good results.

In the meantime, I had to get my game face on.

It would be good to start with this pilot, Luke. Fake it 'til you make it.

Forcing a smile on my face, I watched for Luke.

Surprisingly, it was only a few minutes before he came out of the terminal rolling my two red suitcases along next to him, one in each hand.

I hadn't even allowed myself to think about what I would have done without my luggage. But the huge sense of relief told me enough.

His efficiency made my fake smile a little less fake.

4

LUKE

*S*arah's luggage had not been hard to find. It had been sitting there next to the luggage claim conveyor belt. But that was something I would not tell her.

This girl fell into an entirely different category of travelers. Difficult.

And there was nothing pilots hated more than a difficult passenger.

I was not a fan of west Texas. It was always windy. Fortunately it was October, so it wasn't quite as hot. Still not Fall, but that was typical Texas.

I stowed her luggage away, then climbed back inside the airplane, pulled up the stairs, and secured the door.

Difficult or not, I needed to harness her in.

As I approached her, she smiled at me and I just stopped dead in my tracks, every thought leaving my head.

She was stunning when she was vexed, but this was a whole different level of stunningness.

She had one of those perfect heart shaped faces that graced the magazines that men loved. Red lips that made a man think about all night long kisses. Green eyes that a man could fall into and never come out.

All framed by perfectly highlighted long brunette hair. Thick, straight, and smooth with just a little messy flip at the ends.

When she lifted a delicate eyebrow, I remembered to breathe. Then I remembered that I needed to harness her in.

Passengers who flew commercial didn't know how to harness in.

Harnessing her in required getting close to her.

I took a step closer and the scent of magnolia enveloped me. Magnolia mixed with something else I couldn't quite identify. Whatever it was, it was most definitely feminine.

"I need to harness you in," I said, not sure if I was talking to her or myself.

"I can do it," she said, holding up the belts. And like most passengers, unfamiliar with private jets, she had them crossed.

"I'll help," I said, pulling myself back to reality.

Moving closer, I took one of the straps and untwisted it before snapping it in place. Then did the next one. Still not meeting her gaze, though I could feel her watching me, I tightened the straps equally on both sides.

"How does that feel?" I asked, looking into those green eyes that were hard to look away from. I'd known that would be the case. Yet I'd looked into her eyes anyway.

I'm pretty sure I almost kissed her right then and there, but the control tower called out, giving me clearance to take off.

"It feels fine," she said as I took a backwards step away from her.

Not quite feeling steady, I nonetheless managed to get myself to the pilot's seat and sat down.

Putting the headset on, I confirmed, then buckled myself in.

I taxied toward the runway, heading straight into the sun.

That was exactly what looking in her eyes had been like.

Billionaire's Unexpected Landing 13

Like looking into the sun even when I knew it was dangerous to do so.

"Ready for takeoff," I said into the microphone.

As the wheels left the ground, I had that little catch in my gut that came every time I left the ground.

Yet all I could think about was Sarah. She'd hijacked my thoughts and I'd just met her.

Whoever this Sarah Lawrence was, she was trouble.

5

SARAH

*A*s the wheels left the ground, I sat back and closed my eyes. I slipped my feet out of my shoes to give them a rest, even though I knew that it wasn't going to help in the long run.

This was going to be a short flight to Houston, so I didn't have time to get any work done. Even if I did have time, I wouldn't have been able to focus.

My little plan to put on my game face had backfired. My smile had won over a lot of clients and I knew it.

But this time I wasn't sure who had been won over.

The pilot, Luke Worthington, had smelled so subtly masculine. No cologne. Just soap and maybe shampoo. And maybe he had the faint scent of jet fuel about him, mixed in there somewhere. When had I started finding jet fuel sexy?

He'd been wearing dark glasses, so I hadn't been able to see his eyes. Yet I *felt* him looking at me. It was a little disconcerting to know I was being studied and not being able to see his eyes.

His lips had been so close to mine, they had almost

Billionaire's Unexpected Landing 15

connected of their own accord, pulled together like two magnets.

That wasn't possible, I told myself as we leveled off in the cloudless sky.

Luke had made a smooth take off, but it was the landing that would tell the tale.

Landing was where the new pilots tripped up.

I had never studied aviation and even I knew these things. Of course, I was a frequent flyer, so I had studied from a passenger's perspective.

I needed to focus on my upcoming interview. Even though it wasn't officially until morning, it unofficially started tonight.

I actually had a red cocktail dress packed in my luggage, but I had no time to change into it.

It was probably just as well.

These cocktail party dinners could be tricky. It was a cross between a cocktail party and an interview. Really, it could go either way, so I would be fine in my business skirt, jacket, and heels. My feet would be killing me by the end of the evening, but that was the way of things. If I had known I'd be walking around airports and tarmacs, I would have worn sneakers and carried my heels in my carryon bag.

With that settled in my head, I moved back to the issue at hand.

Sexy pilot.

Zachary would say I've been working too much and not dating. *All work and no play and all that.* One of his favorite sayings. Like he was one to talk.

But he did have a life. A husband and a kid.

I didn't have time to find someone to date, much less actually date.

It was unethical for me to mix business with pleasure. So that meant that all the eligible men I met through my work were off-limits.

And there was no lack of men that under other circumstances, I would have jumped to date.

So… since I worked long hours, I didn't run into anyone eligible for dating.

Sure I'd done the swipe right, swipe left thing, but that just left me feeling hollow. Maybe I was old fashioned. I wanted to meet someone the organic way. I just didn't trust social profiles. Too many people lied. Or at least misrepresented themselves.

Right now I did not have time to have my thoughts clouded with thoughts of the sexy pilot in the sexy pilot's uniform with an oddly sexy hat on his head.

He was more annoying than anything else. He'd taken his time when I was in a hurry and he'd told me not to worry.

As I sat here and calmed my heart rate, I knew it was good that one of us had been calm. Otherwise my luggage would still be sitting in Abilene. And that would have been a disaster. I would have had to wear this same outfit tonight and tomorrow. As it was, I was already mixed up.

I was wearing a black business suit to a dinner party and a red suit to the presentation.

Wearing the red suit didn't bother me so much. It was well-known trick to get men's attention and since eighty-five percent of my clients were men, I knew it worked.

Zachary was smart that way. He assigned me to the male doctors and a guy to the female doctors.

Hey. It wasn't a situation of my doing. I just used what was at my disposal.

I heard the pilot, Luke talking into his microphone. I couldn't hear his words, but the masculine tenor of his voice sent little shivers down my spine.

How long had I been without a man? Three months? Four? Maybe longer. I really couldn't remember. Maybe a year, but who was counting.

Billionaire's Unexpected Landing   17

I could just see his profile when he turned just so. He had a strong jaw and smooth skin. His movements were confident.

I felt safe flying with him.

It occurred to me that we were alone up here in the air. Even though we were both firmly locked into our respective seats, there was something oddly intimate about it.

Maybe there was something to this way of flying. I'd have to talk to Zachary. Of course, I already knew there was no way he would spring for it. He cringed at first class tickets, but knew it was necessary for the image we needed to project.

The flight went far more quickly than I had expected.

As we started our descent, I was oddly disappointed.

What the hell?

I had wanted to get to Houston as quickly as possible.

And now I didn't want the flight to end. How messed up was that?

I distracted myself by composing a text to Zachary that I couldn't send until we were on the ground.

ME: *Just landed in Houston. No time for hotel. Going straight to dinner.*

I sat there and held my phone, watching as the ground came closer and closer. I could see the houses with their swimming pools. The freeway. The mall.

People below with normal lives. Houses with swimming pools. For me it was one of those someday things.

Someday I'd have a house in the suburbs with a swimming pool. Maybe a dog outside and couple of cats in the house.

In the meantime, I lived in my condo in Los Angeles. I was hardly ever there. Sometimes it seemed like it was just a place to relax on the weekends. After my errands.

I certainly couldn't have a pet with my schedule.

But I loved my job. And I wanted to move up the corporate ladder. My ambitions had no limits.

So I had to put off the family. The house. The pets.

My gaze was drawn back to Luke.

Instead of looking outside, I watched him as we came in for a landing. A perfect landing.

I was impressed.

Luke Worthington was one of those men who were good at what they did.

If I had time, I might like to get to know him better.

Even if he did annoy me.

6

LUKE

I was good at landings. It was barely noticeable when the wheels touched the ground.

Takeoffs and landings were my favorite parts of flying simply because they presented the most difficult challenges. When other pilots had been flying from airport to airport, I had been practicing takeoffs and landings.

That's what it took to be good at something. Practice and persistence.

I had no limit to my willingness to practice and no limit to my persistence.

Today I was particularly pleased with my landing simply because I wanted to impress Sarah Lawrence.

I knew nothing about her.

And during that part of the flight when there was little to do, I had invented a history for her. It was just something I did.

She was a recent college graduate. Marketing, of course. She was on her way to a conference. Meeting friends for drinks tonight. That was one theory.

I had a couple of others, but I liked that one best. For some reason, I wanted to think of her as someone who was worried about being late for a fun reason, not anything serious.

I taxied along the runway, feeling the urge to slow down time.

It made no sense. It wasn't like she and I were having a conversation or anything. I just liked having her here in my plane.

I shook my head.

I had plenty of woman. A pilot tended to attract women. They were drawn to the uniform and the prestige.

I'd learned the hard way to keep my distance. A woman who was drawn to the uniform first didn't interest me. I wanted a woman who found me interesting as a man.

Besides, my lifestyle did not lend itself to a stable, long-term relationship.

Women may be drawn to pilots at first, but then when the reality of us being gone all the time sank in, they no longer liked it.

So I wasn't actively looking for anyone to date right now. One could even say that I was avoiding relationships if one wanted to.

However, if someone happened to waltz into my life, I would not be opposed.

Sarah Lawrence was not a good someone. I didn't even know where she was from. She could be from west Texas, God help her.

Though I had to admit that she did not have a west Texas accent.

But the main negative thing about her was her difficulty.

She was too much in a hurry.

My job was just to get her off this plane, to the private terminal, then I could be on my own way.

I still had time to make dinner with my brother and his girlfriend.

Billionaire's Unexpected Landing 21

I secured the plane and unbuckled my seatbelt.

By the time I had everything secured, I fully expected her to be up and standing at the door.

But instead, she had her head bent over her phone, suddenly seemingly in no hurry.

I waited, just enjoying looking at her.

She saw me watching her and slipped on her shoes.

My gut clenched. Something about seeing her out of her shoes was oddly erotic.

She grabbed her bag and stood up. She had seemed taller earlier, when she had been vexed. Now I saw that she was actually a head shorter than I was... or would have been without the heels.

Her expression was troubled, but I was pretty sure it was not directed at me this time.

"Trouble?" I asked.

"There are no Ubers available and no taxis." She looked up at me from beneath long dark lashes. "I may have to rent a car, but..."

"But it takes too long."

She shrugged. "No yeah."

The west coast. That's where she was from. I'd heard that expression before. My cousins said *no yeah and yeah no* all the time.

Somehow it made me feel better about her knowing that she was not doomed to being from West Texas.

"There's always transportation," I said. Wasn't there? Most of my passengers either used their cars or had drivers. It was rare for me to have anyone who needed to call an Uber when they landed.

"Well," she said, her brow furrowed. "There isn't at the moment."

"Where are you needing to go?" I asked.

She named a restaurant in Uptown.

"I can drive you," I said.

Where the hell had that come from? I wasn't a driver. I was her pilot.

She was obviously perplexed by the offer as well, but I could see that she was considering it.

"Okay," she said.

"Okay?"

Now I was going to be late.

"I don't want to put you out," she said. "If you have somewhere you need to be."

Of course I had somewhere to be. Who didn't?

"It's not a problem," I said.

I pulled out my own phone. Sent a quick text to my cousin and opened the door.

As was customary, for me at least, I went down the stairs first so I could assist her at the bottom. I'd had a woman, also wearing heels, trip one time. Lesson learned.

Always go first in order to help the lady down the steep stairs.

When I reached the ground, I turned and held out my hand.

She stopped and looked at me for a moment, then put her hand in mine.

A jolt, like an electrical current, ran through me.

What was it about this girl that had me so twisted up?

I had a rule about dating passengers. Actually it wasn't so much a rule so much as it was something that had just never come up. So I claimed it. It had saved me a few times from some of those women who found pilots attractive.

When she was safely on the tarmac, I released her hand.

Together, in silence, we walked across the tarmac and went inside the Skye Travels terminal.

"I just need to go upstairs for a minute," I said as we reached the elevator.

"I'll wait down here," she said.

Billionaire's Unexpected Landing 23

Not a chance.

"Come on up," I said, holding the elevator for her.

This was a whole other thing. This was about her being someone that my father had personally requested I pick up at the last minute.

I wasn't about to leave her hanging out downstairs.

Since I did not know who she was, I had to assume she was someone my father knew.

And that was a whole other thing.

7

SARAH

I kept reminding myself that I was going to be late.

But since Luke was going to drive me to the restaurant, I didn't have to waste time waiting on transportation. So that gave me an extra few minutes.

And it would have been rude to not give him a minute to do whatever it was he had to do.

We stepped off the elevator in the elegant Skye Travels office. I knew what it was immediately due to the same red logo splashed across the tail of the plane.

I was quite impressed by the modern design.

The elevator opened up into a large lobby area with a receptionist sitting behind a large circular desk.

She smiled as we approached and I realized with a start that she wasn't smiling at us, but she was smiling at Luke.

I saw this all the time in hospitals and clinics. It never surprised me. After all, the doctors that I worked with typically handsome men. A lot of women had a thing for doctors.

But somehow when this woman smiled at Luke I found it... disconcerting.

Billionaire's Unexpected Landing   25

Maybe it was because he didn't fall under my rules of men who were off-limits.

I had no rules against dating pilots or any men outside of my clients and coworkers, for that matter.

Or maybe what was most disconcerting was the way he removed his sunglasses and smiled back.

That was most certainly it. I instantly berated myself. I was here for a job interview.

And this man was kind enough to give me a ride... in his own private vehicle.

I was not here on a date.

"Good evening, Mr. Worthington," the receptionist said.

"Good evening, Abigail," he said, smoothly. "Is my father back there?"

"Yes, sir," she said. "I'll let him know you're here." She picked up the phone receiver.

"No need," Luke said shaking his head. "I'll only be a minute." He was already headed down the hallway.

The woman, Abigail, set the phone receiver down. She looked after Luke, her expression a bit uncertain.

"Hi," she said, noticing me for the first time.

"Hi," I said.

Abigail was a young woman, probably a college student.

She seemed to catch herself. "Can I get you something?" she asked.

I shook my head.

"Water?" she asked.

And suddenly I was incredibly thirsty. I usually picked up a bottle of water on my way out of the airport, but my routine was thrown off.

"Yes, please," I said. "Water would be wonderful."

Abigail got up and went behind a little wall behind her desk and promptly came back with a bottle of water.

"You can have a seat," she said, handing me the bottle.

"Thank you." I took the bottle of water and sat down on one of the little sofas.

Opening the water, I drank half of it.

Then I put the lid back on and studied the label. It was quite understated. Just a two-inch strip in white with the words *Worthington Enterprises.*

Worthington.

I looked over at Abigail. Everything else I'd seen so far had said Skye Travels.

I stood up and walked back over to the desk. Held up the water bottle.

"Who is Worthington Enterprises?" I asked.

Abigail, for the first time, smiled in my direction. "Worthington Enterprises owns Skye Travels." I could see the pride in her expression.

"I see," I said. "Thank you."

I went back to my spot on the sofa and sat back down.

It seems I was in more trouble than I had thought.

My pilot was not just Luke Worthington.

He was Luke *Worthington.*

And if I were a betting woman, I would have put all my money on Luke Worthington being more than just a pilot.

He was somehow part of Worthington Enterprises.

I sipped my water and tried to force my thoughts back on my upcoming interview.

It wasn't happening.

All I could think about was the handsome Luke Worthington and how right my hand had felt in his.

8

LUKE

I stepped into Father's office without bothering to knock. As always, he looked a bit annoyed. That was Quinn Worthington's typical expression, so it didn't deter me in the least.

"What's up?" he asked, looking up from his computer.

I stood in front of him and crossed my arms. "I'm supposed to meet Daniel and his girlfriend for dinner," I said, but I'm not going to make it."

"Why not?" he asked, pulling off his reading glasses.

"The passenger... the young lady you had me pick up in Abilene needs a ride to Uptown."

"Okay," he shrugged. "What does one have to do with the other?"

"Well," I said. "I'm supposed to meet Daniel across the street at the Sky House, but the girl you had me pick up needs me to drive her."

Father shook his head. "I just made the call."

"What do you mean?"

"The request came down from Grandpa. I'm just the one who called you."

"Oh," I said. My grandpa, Noah Worthington was the founder of Skye Travels and he was legendary.

"So anyway, since I can't meet Daniel, I was thinking maybe you'd want to."

Father looked at me like I had suddenly sprouted wings and asked why he didn't have any.

"Okay," I said, tapping the back of one of the leather chairs in front of his desk. "I'll just tell Daniel that none of us are available."

"Ask your brother," he said.

"Don't have time," I said over my shoulder. "I'm making my passenger late just standing here."

"Then why are you even here?" he asked as I walked out.

"Keys," I said, mumbling to myself as I walked down the hallway and slipped into the office where the car keys were kept.

This was the downside of having too much going on.

A driver had picked me up that morning from my apartment because my car was being serviced.

So I didn't have my car. And I wasn't about to call for a car. Instead I was just going to take one of the company cars.

It was better if I didn't let Sarah know who I was until I found out who she was. Another one of those hard learned lessons.

I grabbed the key fob to the plain black BMW SUV and slipped it into my pocket.

At first I didn't see Sarah.

She was sitting on one of the sofas, typing on her phone.

Just like everyone else, I thought.

She stood up when she saw me and I knew something was different.

She had a bottle of water in her hand.

The Worthington Enterprises water my Aunt Brianna had insisted we try. She was all about image. She was, in fact, the one who had designed the original Skye Travels logos. They had changed over the years, of course, to stay up with the times, but her touch was still on everything.

"Ready?" I asked with a grin. This girl was a smart one. She'd put things together really quickly.

Fortunately, it didn't really bother me that she knew I had the Worthington name. I was merely the boss's son anyway.

9

SARAH

"Sure," I said, falling into step beside Luke.

As we passed a wastebasket near the elevator, I tossed the empty water bottle into it.

"Are you sure this isn't an inconvenience?" I asked. "I checked again and there's an Uber that can be here in fifteen."

"We're well on our way already," he said, pressing the elevator button.

"Alright," I said, keeping my gaze straight ahead.

We rode in silence down the elevator.

By the time we were outside again, it was dark.

Cars flew by on the highway outside the building, their headlights lighting up the parking lot.

The car beeped and Luke opened the passenger door for me.

As I stepped past, my gaze caught his and I froze.

Looking into his magnetic blue eyes, seeing them for the first time, had the same effect on me that putting my hand in his had.

It was like a jolt of electricity shooting through me.

After a second that felt more like a minute, I slipped into

Billionaire's Unexpected Landing 31

the passenger seat of the new BMW and he closed the door.

Seconds later, he came around and climbed into the driver's seat.

When he smiled over at me, my breath snagged.

Good heavens. I straightened in my seat.

I was not a school girl on a first date.

Though apparently, my body didn't know it.

I hadn't felt this was since... well... ever. I recognized the feeling from my prom night, but that had been such a disaster, it didn't bear remembering.

He spoke the name of my restaurant into the GPS and we were off.

"We'll be there in forty-two minutes," he said. "Will that make you late?"

"I don't think so," I said. Actually I had sent a message to Zach letting him know I had a transportation problem. And he had let the President of the company know.

The stars appeared to have aligned for me tonight because the company President was also running late.

So, it seemed, no one cared, after all. Tyler Lexton would be sitting there along with everyone else. Waiting.

Luke pulled out in the traffic, seemingly driving as smoothly as he flew.

"Nice landing," I said. "earlier."

He grinned. "You noticed."

"Of course," I said, smiling back.

And just like that I had my game face back on.

I knew how to make people feel important. I did it all the time.

"You must really enjoy flying," I said.

"It's the best job a person could possibly have," he said, getting onto the freeway.

I knew from his voice that he believed that with every fiber of his being.

10

LUKE

I was a little confused by Sarah.

When I met her at the Abilene airport, she had been dead set against being late. Now she seemed relaxed and unconcerned.

Maybe she had reconciled herself to being late and it no longer bothered her.

I'd been like that before.

When worrying about something no longer helped, a person could just relax.

"Headed to a conference?" I asked. As soon as I asked it, I realized I should have just asked her outright what she was doing in Houston. I should not have thrown out my wild speculations that had no basis in reality.

Her expression told me that I way off base this time, but she didn't bother to correct me.

"Something like that," she said.

Encouraged, I went ahead with my little theory. What the hell?

"Marketing?" I asked.

"You're a bit too close for comfort," she said.

Billionaire's Unexpected Landing   33

I laughed.

"I'm not even close, am I?"

She looked ahead, watching as I maneuvered around traffic. The BMW did about half the driving, so I could watch her, too.

"Yeah. No," she said. "I'm here for an interview."

"I was off base," I said.

She shook her head, then turned back to me and smiled. "But I do have a degree in marketing."

"No kidding?" I asked.

"No kidding."

"I guess I am that good," I said.

"And not a little bit modest either."

I grinned.

I liked this Sarah Lawrence.

She was fun to be around.

"How long are you in town for this interview?"

"I leave day after tomorrow."

"Back to west Texas?" I asked, knowing the answer already.

"God, no," she said with a little shiver.

"I was right about that, too."

"Is that so?" she asked. "You think you've got me all figured out."

"I've been right, so far," I said.

"Alright," she said, crossing her arms. "Give me your best shot."

"Really?" I asked, changing lanes to get around a traffic jam.

"Yes," she said with a little grin. "I'm curious what you think."

"Okay." I straightened in my seat. "Let's see. You're from L.A."

"What did you do? Google me?" She narrowed her eyes at me.

"When would I have time to do that?" I glanced over at her. "So am I right?" I grinned.

"Yes. How did you know?"

"I have cousins in L.A. You talk like them." And it was a really lucky guess. I knew where her flight had originated.

She laughed. "Alright. Fair enough. What else?"

Since she was going to an interview, I had been wrong about the whole meeting friends for drinks at a conference thing.

But I was not to be deterred.

"I think you're a recent college graduate," I said.

"I'm not as young as I look."

I studied her from the corner of my eye. She did look young, but she didn't hold herself like a youngster. She held herself with the confidence of a professional.

"I can see that," I said. "You're good at your job, whatever it is."

"You don't want to venture a guess?" I heard the teasing tone in her voice.

"Well, now you're trying to make me look bad."

She shrugged. "Maybe."

I concentrated on traffic to give myself time to think.

She was not a high level executive because I was pretty sure she'd never flown private before.

"You're thinking too hard," she said.

"Ah ha," I said.

"Ah ha what?"

"You're in mental health."

The smile faded from her lips.

I was pretty sure I had her this time.

11

SARAH

*E*verything was fun and games until it got real.

How could Luke Worthington possibly be right?

The traffic picked up as we neared the restaurant. I knew we were near because I could see the GPS from here.

Looked like our forty-two minutes was going to stretch a little longer.

So far Houston reminded me a bit of L.A., mostly because it was a big city, but it had a different feel to it already.

Oddly enough, it felt more urban.

As we slowed to a near stop, a car pulled up next to us, music blaring. A universal thing, it seemed.

"So am I right?" Luke asked.

"You're actually more right than not."

"So I'm close?"

He was too close. If it was that obvious what I did, perhaps I needed to be a bit more careful when I traveled.

"Mental health?"

"How could you know that?"

He shrugged. "Several of my family members are psychologists. My grandmother. Two of my aunts."

"Oh," I said, relaxing a little bit. He'd been exposed to people in mental health, so he had picked up a few of the techniques. The speech patterns. Just as I had.

"Again," I said. "Sort of." But when he looked at me with disappointment, I knew I had to tell him more.

"I work around mental health professionals." I shrugged. "With them."

Now I had him perplexed.

"Alright," he said. "I got this close. Walk me the rest of the way."

"I work with psychiatrists."

"A counselor," he said, then corrected himself. "No. You said you work around mental health."

I should just tell him already. But this was kinda fun.

"An accountant?"

"God no," I said. "That sounds incredibly boring."

"Agreed."

"You got me."

"I'm a drug rep. Psychotropic drugs."

"Get out," he said.

"Why?"

"My grandmother was a drug rep back in the day. She started out that way, then went to graduate school to become a psychologist."

"How cool is that?" I asked.

"You'd like her," he said. "I'll have to introduce you."

My heart flipped over at his words.

I knew he was just talking. But he had just said he wanted to introduce me to his family.

And that was doing funny things to my emotions.

Mostly because I actually liked the idea.

A little bit too much.

Fortunately, we were exiting the freeway and would be pulling up to the hotel soon.

Billionaire's Unexpected Landing   37

"Thank you for giving me a ride," I said, purposely changing the direction of the conversation. "I hope it wasn't too far out of your way."

"Not at all," he said, but somehow I got the idea that he wasn't being entirely truthful. At least not about that.

12

LUKE

$\mathcal{W}$e were almost to the restaurant where I was dropping Sarah off for what was likely part of her interview. That explained why she had been so upset about being late. Though why that had changed, I really didn't know.

The current problem was that I wasn't ready to let her go.

I still had so much to learn about her. That and I was immensely enjoying her company. She was not only pretty to look at, she was interesting to talk to. That was a combination I seemed to be having trouble finding lately.

Maybe I was becoming jaded with dating. But whatever it was about her, I found myself trying to figure out a way to see her again.

As I pulled up to the restaurant and waved off the valet, I realized that I was trying to be hip, slick, and cool about it.

Sometimes the best way to do something was to just be direct.

I pulled up to the curb and put the car in park.

"I'll come around," I said, as I jumped and came around to her door before the valet could beat me to it.

I opened her door and held out a hand to help her out.

Billionaire's Unexpected Landing   39

She didn't hesitate to put her hand in mine this time. I took that as progress.

I closed her door, but I didn't release her hand.

"You're sure my luggage will end up at my hotel?" she asked, a bit of worry playing about her brow.

"You told the receptionist?"

"Yes."

"Then I'm certain," I said. "we do this all the time."

She nodded.

"I should go," she said. "But she didn't try to pull away. Her feet didn't move.

"I know," I said.

"Am I forgetting something else?" she asked.

I laughed. "Maybe."

She looked at me with curiosity.

"What?"

I took a deep breath and plunged right into the deep end. I normally didn't have a hard time asking women out. In fact, I never had a hard time with it. Mainly because I never cared what their answer was.

But with Sarah, I cared very much what the answer was.

"I want to see you again."

She smiled a slow smile that made me want to kiss her right here and now.

And I might just would have, except that the valet guy came up and asked for my key.

"I'm not staying," I said, trying to keep the annoyance out of my voice.

The valet apologized and darted off to help the next customer.

"I have some time tomorrow," she said, pulling her hand free now.

She walked toward the restaurant, then turned around and

took a step backwards. I was rather impressed by that accomplishment in heels.

"Be at my hotel," she said, turning back around forward again. "At four o'clock."

Then she was striding toward the door to the restaurant.

As I watched the doorman open the door for her, I grinned to myself.

She reminded me very much of my grandmother, Savannah Worthington.

I had some things to figure out.

One, I had to find out where her hotel was. Abigail, the receptionist, would know. And, two, I had to do something about the flight I had scheduled for tomorrow.

Why was it the most interesting women were the hardest to obtain?

It was a phenomenon that was as old as the ages. And yet this was the first time I had ever personally encountered it.

13

SARAH

*A*s I walked into the restaurant, my mind was not on my interview. Not even a little. My mind was squarely on the unexpected date that I had with Luke tomorrow.

I had not come here to go on a date. That had been the last thing on my mind.

But now it was front and center the most important part of my trip.

The smile I wore as I approached the dinner table of the company president and my competition could not have been more genuine.

I soon discovered that the president, Mr. Madris had just gotten here and didn't seem to be the least bit concerned that I was a few minutes late and no one even mentioned it. I'd expected more people here, but it looks like it was only going to be the three of us. Mr. Madris, the company president and Tyler Lexton, my competition. This was quite unusual, but things happened.

Mr. Madris already had one drink and was well into his second. I took one sip of mine, then merely used it as a prop. I needed my mind clear. Or at least as clear as it could be considering that it was full of Luke Worthington.

Even though I didn't want to, I forced myself to tuck him into the back of my mind until after the evening was over. When I was back in my hotel room, I could replay our conversation and think about him all I wanted.

But for right now, I had far too much riding on this evening to not give it my full attention.

Mr. Madris was a pleasant man, though, and it turned out to be easier to do than I expected.

"How do you like Houston?" Mr. Madris asked, stirring the ice in his drink with his finger.

"I only arrived at the airport a few minutes ago," I said. "but so far I like it very much." And not to say anything about the main reason I liked Houston so far was because of a pilot named Luke Worthington.

"How do you like living here?" I asked Tyler.

"I've lived here my whole life," Tyler said, lifting his glass of amber liquid. "I don't think I would consider living anywhere else."

Though I tried to pull Tyler into the conversation, Mr. Madris was still talking to me.

"There's an event tomorrow," he said. "a black tie event. I'd like you to attend." He glanced at Tyler. "You, too, of course."

"What kind of black tie event?" I asked. It didn't really matter. If he wanted me to go, I would go, of course. It was part of the whole interview process.

What I was calculating though, was just how it was going to interfere with my date with Luke. I had figured four o'clock would give me plenty of time to finish up with the required interview activities.

But now it wasn't looking so good. The black tie event would probably start around seven or eight. That only gave me

Billionaire's Unexpected Landing 43

about three hours... no I had to get dressed, so two hours... with Luke.

"It's a charity event," Mr. Madris said. "If you two are going to be moving up the company ladder, you'll need to be there."

Tyler and I both smiled indulgently. Mr. Madris was being purposely obtuse, perhaps, since only one of the two of us was going to be climbing this particular corporate ladder at this time.

There was an additional problem that I had to calculate in. A black tie event meant I needed an evening gown. Since this was supposed to be an interview trip, I had not brought an evening gown. So along with everything else, I had figure out when to go shopping for a suitable dress.

14

LUKE

The building was in shadows when I got back to the office. The lobby lights were off, but the lights were still on in Father's office and he was still at his desk. That could only mean one thing. Mother was out on a flight.

My parents had an interesting arrangement. He ran Skye Travels and had never flown an airplane. My mother had a business degree, but she piloted a flight a couple of times every week.

Since Father was still here, working, that told me that Mother had taken a flight today and wasn't back yet. He always waited here for her when she flew. I couldn't remember a time when he didn't.

I dropped off the keys, then walked quietly past Father's office.

"What are you doing back?" Father asked.

Busted. I turned around and walked into his office.

"Just brought the keys back," I said. "Need to check the schedule."

"Thought you were having dinner with Daniel and his girlfriend."

Billionaire's Unexpected Landing   45

"I had to drop the passenger off, remember?" I said. Sometimes I thought Father's mind was slipping.

"Right," he said, sitting back and looking away from the computer. "Went okay?"

"Of course," I said, not willing to tell him just how well it really went.

"Come," he said. "Sit for a minute."

Since I couldn't think of any reason not to, I sat in one of the two chairs in front of his desk.

"I cancelled your flight for tomorrow afternoon," he said.

"Alright," I said, keeping my expression blank, but I was doing summersaults on the inside. My father had just saved me the trouble of doing what I'd come back to do.

I could have changed my schedule from my home computer, but I needed to drop the key off anyway.

Then just as quickly, I went on alert.

"Why did you cancel my flight?" I asked.

When a smile flashed across Father's face, I knew I wasn't going to like the reason.

"I need you to attend an event."

"What kind of event?"

"A charity event in River Oaks."

"Why don't you go?" I asked.

"I am going," he said. "We're all going. Your mother. Your grandparents."

Damn.

I had a date with Sarah.

"Why don't you take Dylan?"

Father waved a hand dismissively. "Dylan isn't ready."

"What does that mean?"

I knew what he meant, but I asked anyway. I was a saint compared to my brother. Dylan was a pilot, too, but when he wasn't flying, he was partying.

My parents called him their wild child.

Still. It should not excuse Dylan from his social obligations.

A man didn't get to carry the Worthington name without certain obligations.

Unless, you were Dylan Worthington.

But for whatever reason, my parents didn't hold my brother responsible.

"At any rate, I cancelled your flight, so you can be at the event."

I bit my tongue. I was supposed to meet Sarah at four o'clock.

"What time do I have to be there?" I asked.

"Six o'clock."

Six o'clock.

I was meeting Sarah at four. Allowing for traffic, I was going to have all of about one hour to spend with Sarah.

Maybe things were not looking up quite as much as I had thought.

15

SARAH

I took an Uber to my hotel. It was such a short distance I was certain I could have walked it, but since I didn't know Houston, it made more sense to use transportation.

The evening had gone longer than I had planned. Everything did, of course. It was one of those laws of life. But I needed sleep so I could get up in the morning and make my presentation.

After I checked in, the clerk went into the back and brought out my two red suitcases.

They were there just as Luke had promised.

So far Skye Travels was an impressive company.

A few minutes later, after I found my room, I stepped out of my heels and sat on the edge of the bed.

I held my phone in my hands. The evening had gone well, all in all. I felt a little bad for Tyler. Mr. Madris had talked to me far more than he had Tyler. But then, Tyler was from here, so if I had to guess, I'd say they already knew each other.

I would also bet money that Mr. Madris already knew which one of us he was going to choose for the promotion.

Aside from all that, there was the other problem—the more pressing one.

I had made a date with Luke.

A date I wasn't going to be able to keep.

I should have known better.

This was an interview trip. Not a pleasure trip.

The two never mixed.

I still had to meet him downstairs at the hotel at four tomorrow.

It would not be right to stand him up and I had no way to get in touch with him.

Unless...

I unlocked my phone and googled Skye Travels.

Founded by Noah Worthington. Expanded into Worthington Enterprises to include aviation and architecture and a number of other ventures.

It did not take long for pictures to populate on the screen.

I went to the website and a page of handsome pilots, some female even, came right up.

A few more clicks and there it was.

Luke Worthington. On the board of directors of Skye Travels.

Son of Quinn Worthington—the President. Grandson of Noah Worthington—the founder and CEO of everything.

Well hell.

I laid back on the bed and let my phone fall to my side.

I had managed to not only stumble onto a date with a pilot, but the son of the owner's family.

According to what I'd read so far, he might as well be royalty in the aviation world. And if he wasn't a billionaire, he was certainly the son of one.

I was around wealthy psychiatrists all the time. But this was a whole new level.

At least I knew how to get in touch with him.

Billionaire's Unexpected Landing 49

All I had to do was to call the number on my phone and leave a message for him.

Maybe tomorrow.

Right now I needed some sleep.

And tomorrow I had to be up, bright-eyed and ready for my presentation.

Tomorrow I would figure it all out.

16

LUKE

I switched lanes, zipping through traffic like it was sitting still. If a man had to drive a car, he had to drive a sports car. There was no other way to compensate for transporting on the ground.

I had my fire-engine red Maserati Quattroporte back from its routine service and all was good. Eighties music, the last of the real music before everything went techno, streamed through my speakers.

It might be October, but this was Houston. The air conditioning blasted through the vents.

Since I lived in a high rise condo in River Oaks, it was nothing to zip over to Uptown to Sarah's hotel. Being a native Houston, I'd mentally calculated in the additional time for traffic.

Finding her hotel had been simple enough. I just asked the delivery guy who dropped off her luggage.

I'd done that first thing this morning, then dropped a passenger off in Dallas, then home to shower and change into my black tuxedo. It might be a little off to wear a tuxedo on a first date, but a man did what he had to do.

Billionaire's Unexpected Landing   51

I glanced at the GPS. After all that, I was still going to be an hour early.

I passed by the Worthington Enterprises building. One of the newest in the area. Centrally located. A Skye Travels office on the twelfth floor. We had our board meeting here, but other than that I rarely went into this building except when I wanted to see Grandpa. No need. Since I was a pilot, I used the office north of town at the airport.

After pulling up to the front of the hotel, I gave my keys to the valet and strode through the lobby.

There was a large two-floor waterfall in the center of the lobby. I looked a bit more like something one would see in an airport than a hotel.

I rode up the escalator to the second floor and stood looking over the balcony.

From here I could see everything.

The hotel wasn't crowded this time of day. If there had been a morning conference, all evidence was picked up and hidden away.

I wondered why they put Sarah here. A smaller, more intimate place would have seemed more appropriate to put a girl for a job interview.

Maybe it was close to the company offices.

There had to be a reason and that was as good as any. But that was me, always trying to figure things out.

People said I took after my grandmother in that way. And I took after my grandfather in both my affinity for and skill with flying.

So I liked to think I was a perfect combination of the two of them. It didn't bother me that I skipped taking after my father. I got along okay with my mother. But it was my grandparents that I was close to.

A couple, a young man and a young woman walked passed and got onto the escalator. Their heads were bent together talking about something, then they laughed. The man looked to be too old for her.

I took him for a colleague or a friend until he put his arm across her shoulders and she leaned into him just before they got off the escalator.

They were most definitely more than friends.

I checked my phone. I still had another thirty minutes.

I moved along so I was standing over the waterfall and looked down, watching the water plummet into the pool below.

If this hotel hadn't been built years ago, I would have thought maybe it was one of my cousin's designs.

Sometimes it felt like I was related to half of Houston. Maybe just the half I associated with.

I sat on a bench behind a large leafy plant and checked my messages.

I had a text confirming my flight in the morning.

Skye Travels was busy, I'd give them that.

I was thinking I could just make a showing at the fundraiser. Be seen. Then slip out.

I'd ask Sarah to wait for me.

Then we would have the rest of the evening to ourselves.

Her flight out was scheduled in the morning. That hadn't been hard to find out either.

I adjusted my cuffs. She would be here anytime.

17

SARAH

"Come on," Mr. Madris said. "I want to show the two of you where your office will be."

Tyler and I looked at each other as we followed Mr. Madris down the hallway.

He couldn't seem to quite grasp the reality that we were competing against each other.

I hadn't decided if it was because he was getting up in age or if he was just eccentric. Perhaps a touch of both.

Either way, we followed him down a quiet hallway to a corner office.

He proudly opened the door and we walked through.

It was a nice office. A nice corner office. What every young professional dreamed of. It had a desk, but otherwise was unfurnished. Furnishing it was probably one of the perks of the job.

But right now, all I was dreaming of was finding a way to escape so I could meet Luke.

Shifting so that I could look out the window at the view over the city, I stole a glance at my watch.

I was going to be late.

That seemed to be the theme of the last two days. But, I reminded myself. Everything would work out. It always did. There was no need to unduly stress.

Turning, I smiled at Mr. Madris.

"This is a lovely office," I said. "Do you mind excusing me for a bit? I have an errand to take care of before tonight's event."

Mr. Madris's look of disappointment was momentary and I might even have imagined it.

He waved his hand. "Of course," he said. "Do what you need to do."

As I walked past him, he lowered his voice.

"They tell me Nordstrom is a good place to shop."

I grinned. Mr. Madris really was a likeable man. It made this job all the more attractive.

Feeling the first brush of freedom I'd had all day, I quickly found myself to the elevator. The company building was fifteen minutes from my hotel.

I pressed the button and stared at my watch. I had all of sixteen minutes to meet Luke.

Since I hadn't gotten around to calling his office, I was going to have to cancel our date in person. Not the most conventional procedure. But it wasn't the most conventional situation.

As I'd gone through the day, I'd accepted that I didn't want to call and cancel. I wanted to see him again. Even if it was only for a few minutes.

So... I had to call an Uber to get to the hotel, find Luke, then call another Uber to take me to Nordstrom and find a dress. A quick search told me it was in the Galleria which wasn't far from the hotel.

At least everything was within ten minutes of everything else. Another of advantage of working here was the central location. In L.A. everything was far more scattered.

Billionaire's Unexpected Landing 55

I pressed elevator button again, knowing full well it had nothing to do with how fast it arrived.

Then finally, the doors opened and I stepped inside the elevator. Seven floors down to the lobby.

I used the time to schedule an Uber. It would be here shortly. Or so they said.

My heels clicked across the deserted bottom floor of the building. I smiled at the doorman as he held the door for me.

I paced toward the circle drive, then back again.

"Can I help you with anything?" the doorman asked.

"Just waiting for an Uber."

"Let me know if you need anything," he said. Stepping back inside out of the sun.

I should probably go back inside, too, but the sun was warm on my skin after spending a day inside the air-conditioned building.

To keep from causing the doorman to worry, I wondered over to a wrought-iron bench in a little outside sitting area.

I had a completely different view of the building from here.

When a bronze plaque on the side of the building snagged my attention, I stood up again and wandered over to look at it, stopping right in front of it.

Worthington Enterprises.

That was it. And a date. No other explanation.

Well that could be anything. Maybe Worthington Enterprises was an investor.

Big companies had a tendency to stick together.

Before I had time to think much more about it, my Uber came up the circle drive.

And I was off and running.

18

LUKE

She wasn't coming.

I tried to remember the last time I had been stood up.

I came up with never.

And I was proud to say that I had never stood anyone up either.

I had to give Sarah the benefit of the doubt. Since she had been here for an interview, she had gotten tied up.

It would be impossible to tell a potential employer that you needed to leave so you could meet a guy you met yesterday.

I tapped my fingers against my watch as I calculated just how long I could stay before I had to leave to make the event.

Father wanted me there early. Maybe I could sidestep on that a bit. He hadn't said why he wanted me there early. No doubt some kind of family thing since both my parents and grandparents were going to be there.

I had a previous engagement. Besides, a better offer was a better offer.

People came and went. I waited until four forty-five.

She wasn't coming.

Billionaire's Unexpected Landing   57

It was okay. Stalling a little bit more, I put the address for the fundraising event in my GPS. It was forty-five minutes away.

Damn it. Something had happened with traffic. It was supposed to only be fifteen minutes from here.

It was time to hang it up.

Grandma would say it wasn't meant to be.

I loved the story of how she and Grandpa had gotten together. They had dated in college, then Grandpa had married someone else. That part was a little muddy for me. It had apparently been back in the day when marriages were still made for business reasons.

At any rate, years later, right after Grandpa got divorced, he and Grandma had happened across each other in a busy airport.

Following merely clues, he'd tracked her all the way to New York and the rest of history.

There was more to the story, but that was the gist of it.

Grandma believed that when something was supposed to happen, it would. No amount of wishing or rushing something could make it happen.

So with that firmly in my mind, I went back down the escalator and retrieved my Maserati.

At least Father would be happy tonight.

As I drove down Westheimer, I saw what was clogging the traffic. An accident had the entire east-bound and west-bound lanes closed. As soon as I saw it, I made a quick detour down one of the side roads.

It was fortunate I knew this part of town like the back of my hand.

A text came up on my screen.

FATHER: *Are you close? We're in the Skyline Lounge.*

No, I'm not close. Whatever it was, I hoped it was important.

I dictated a message back.

ME: *Caught in traffic. Will be there shortly.*

There. He could verify that on his Citizen app if he wanted to. He did not need to know that I had waited forty-five minutes for my date to show up.

Although I told myself I should stop thinking about her, my gut told me that she had not done it on purpose.

19

SARAH

The traffic was horrendous. Some of the worst I had ever seen.

"Do you know any way around it?" I asked my driver.

"Si," he said," holding up his hands. "But stuck."

"Right. Stuck."

It was already forty-five minutes after four. Even if Luke had shown up to the hotel, he wouldn't be there now.

I tried to focus on the interview. I felt like it had gone well enough. My presentation had gone off without a hitch. Mr. Madris had spent a large amount of his day with us. And despite the competition, I liked Tyler. I think he and I could have been friends under other circumstances. And maybe we could be anyway after this interview business was over.

My time was running close. With the traffic backed up like this, there was no way I was going to make it to the hotel, make it to Nordstrom, buy a dress, and get back to the event.

I pulled up the GPS and checked our location.

We were coming up on the intersection where we would need to turn one way for the hotel and another for the department store.

Then finally, I saw the reason for the delay. A wrecker, carrying a smashed in car, passed us.

I had to be reasonable. I should have called the Skye Travels number already to get a message to Luke.

Since I had it saved in my contacts, I pulled it up, took a deep breath, and dialed it.

Voicemail.

Now there was no way to get a message to Luke.

It was time to call it.

"Change of plans," I said out loud.

"You go somewhere different?"

"Yes," I said. "Please take me to Nordstrom instead."

"Si," the driver said. "I take you to Nordstrom's."

"Thank you," I said, sitting back and blowing out a breath. It was an unfortunate turn of events. That's what it was. I had spent all night and all day. Twenty-four hours, practically, thinking about Luke Worthington.

And now I wasn't even going to see him again. I was leaving in the morning, heading back to L.A.

I consoled myself that IF I got the job with Clinical Pharm, I would be moving here and I could look him up then.

Somehow that just felt wrong.

It was something I couldn't see myself doing.

If I came to work here, I would be focusing on work, not looking up a guy I had met on a plane. Even if he was the pilot.

A few minutes later, the driver pulled up in front of Nordstrom and I went inside.

It only took a couple of minutes to figure where the formal gowns were.

I went up the escalator straight to the dresses.

"Good evening," the salesgirl said. "What can I help you with?"

"I need a dress," I said. "for tonight. For a black-tie event."

"Okay," she said. "Want to look around some?"

Billionaire's Unexpected Landing 61

I glanced at my watch. "I don't really have time," I said. "I'm already running late."

"Right," she said. "Well, let's get started."

And we dove right in. Fortunately, I was a perfect size six, so there were plenty of things on the rack to choose from.

20

LUKE

*F*ather met me outside the Skyline Lounge.

The Skyline Lounge inside the Astorian was a small, private area off the main ballroom. Like the rest of the building, it was elegantly furnished with lush burgundy curtains and matching velvet covered benches.

"There was an accident on Westheimer," I said, trying not to sound defensive. "Not my fault."

Father waved me off. That, in itself, made me suspicious. Father was high strung. Not the kind to just wave things off. Not things that mattered to him.

And he looked preoccupied.

"Is Grandpa in there?" I asked.

"Yes." Father ran a hand through his hair and paced away.

The faint sound of orchestra music drifted from the main ballroom. It was a bit discordant as they were warming up. We'd attended several events at the historical Astorian. It was always elegant and we always met here to go in to the ballroom together.

"What is it Father?" I asked. "Where's Mother?"

"She's inside," he answered distractedly.

Billionaire's Unexpected Landing 63

"We should go in," I said.

"No," he said, turning and pacing back to me.

His eyes were troubled.

"I need to ask you something," he said. "And I'll tell you up front that your grandmother is vehemently opposed to this idea."

"What is it?" I asked. "Are you… firing me?" It was the worst thing I could think of at the moment that he could be up to.

"No," Father said with a little laugh. "Nothing like that. You're an excellent pilot."

"What then?" I went to the door of the lounge and peeked inside. I didn't see anything amiss. My parents and grandparents sitting at a little table, holding champagne glasses.

As a formally dressed waiter walked by with a tray of champagne glasses, Father took two.

"An opportunity has come up," he said, handing one of the flutes to me.

"Opportunities are good," I said.

"Sometimes." He sipped the champagne.

"Father." The flute suddenly felt foreign in my hand. "I'm just going to go—"

"Wait." He put a hand on my arm. "An opportunity has come up for us to merge with the Madris family."

"The Madris family." I had a sinking feeling about this. Though mergers were common in business, they were not common in Worthington Enterprises. Unless there was financial trouble I didn't know about. Father never talked to me about company finances. As far as I knew, the company was in good standing.

"I don't understand. The Madris family already has a floor in our Worthington Enterprises building. What more could they want?"

"Mr. Madris wants to see his granddaughter married."

Now the feeling was more than just sinking. Now it was more like a sickness revolting in my stomach.

"Why are you telling me this?" I asked, narrowing my eyes.

Father smiled a humorless smile.

"Because you're the most likely candidate. Dylan is too wild and your other two brothers are too young."

I turned up the champagne flute and emptied half of it.

"Is Worthington Enterprises in financial trouble?" I asked.

Father looked at me like I was speaking Martian.

"No," he said, not bothering to elaborate.

The tension rose as the seconds passed. I tossed back the rest of my champagne.

"Are you telling me you want me to marry Zoe Madris?"

When Father didn't answer right away, I backed up to one of the velvet covered benches and dropped onto it, my legs no longer wanting to hold me.

"It's the only way," Father said, running a hand over his face. "It's the only way this merger will happen."

To hell with the merger, I thought, but I didn't say it out loud. Not yet anyway.

"What is this, Father?" I asked, not believing this was happening. It felt like something out of the dark ages. "Please help me understand this madness."

21

SARAH

*A*fter the doorman opened the taxi door, I walked up to the front door of the Astorian.

Another doorman smiled as he opened the door.

"Are you having a good night, so far, Miss?" he asked.

"Yes," I said. "Thank you."

I'd had to make some quick choices at Nordstrom's. Normally I would have taken more time on any decision that would take several hundred dollars out of my bank account.

I consoled myself by imagining presenting Zachary with the receipt. I may have jumped at the interview opportunity, but Zachary had orchestrated it.

Of course, I knew I wouldn't do that. Besides, I rather liked the dress and I could realistically wear it again. A perfect fit, I'd worn it right out of Nordstrom's. I'd got some interesting looks, to say the least.

It was a floor length column silhouette dress in a crimson red that I had to admit took a lot of confidence to pull off. The wrap skirt had a cascading ruffle down the left side along with a high slit. The square neckline with delicate straps topped it all off with a clean, elegant finish.

I'd even had time to grab some new red heels from the shoe department. The last thing I needed was another pair of shoes, but the best thing about these was that at the moment, they did not hurt my feet.

The salesgirl had done something amazing to my hair and it had only taken her five minutes. she'd pulled about half of it up onto the top of my head and left the rest down.

I could truly never remember feeling quite so openly sexy.

Of course, feeling sexy was not likely to determine whether or not I got a promotion. But I didn't care.

What I did regret most was that I hadn't gotten the chance to see Luke.

I followed the crowd and the music to the tables set up for the fundraiser.

There were several people available to help get people where they needed to go and it only took a few minutes for me to locate Mr. Madris and Tyler.

Tyler nodded his approval. I subtle nod that I could have easily imagined and he could have easily denied. But I did not imagine it.

"Come," Mr. Madris said. "I want you to meet my granddaughter."

We followed him through the crowd to what was obviously his private table.

A lovely young blonde girl sat at the table between two handsome young men. They were all about the same age. Probably about five years younger than me.

"Zoe," Mr. Madris said. "These are our applicants. Tyler and Sarah."

Zoe smiled. A very controlled smile.

"It's a pleasure to meet you," she said. "These are my friends Beau and Charlie."

"Hello Zoe, Beau, and Charlie." I looked at each one of them in turn.

"Have a seat," Mr. Madris said, pulling out a chair for me. "This completes our table."

I realized I didn't know if there was a Mrs. Madris. I didn't remember seeing anything about her in my Internet search and Zachary hadn't said anything. But I also had not known about his granddaughter.

I knew that Clinical Pharm was a closely held corporation, at the top at least, but it was so spread out at the bottom it didn't have a small corporation feel.

I had expected Mr. Madris to have more of his corporate officers here tonight.

Before I had much time to sort it out, the first speaker asked for our attention.

22

LUKE

My conversation with Father about marrying Zoe Madris was cut short… Thank God… when my grandparents and my mother came out and insisted that we take our seats at our table.

Feeling truly ill, I sat between Grandpa and Mother.

According to Father, no one else knew about this… thing… whatever it was. Arranged marriage? Before I did. Except, apparently Grandma, who had told him to leave it alone. And I was pretty sure she had not told anyone else… yet. She would tell Grandpa when the time was right.

It left me feeling not a little uncomfortable.

As the first speaker droned on, I scanned the audience. I wasn't sure who I was looking for. Zoe maybe.

I'd never known that she was having trouble finding a husband. I'd seen her in passing. Met her at some point. But I never paid her that much attention. She was attractive enough. I knew enough about the family to know that she had a nose job when she was fifteen. I didn't know what else she'd had done after that gateway surgery.

I didn't care enough to keep up.

Billionaire's Unexpected Landing 69

It didn't take much effort to spot her sitting two tables over. Her striking platinum hair stood out in any crowd.

She was sitting between her two friends, Beau and Charlie. And she was wearing a red dress. She actually looked quite good tonight, but not good enough for me to consider dating, much less marrying. Personally, I preferred my women with brunette hair.

I glanced over at my Grandfather. Hadn't he had an arranged marriage before he married Grandma? Surely the two of them wouldn't agree to this.

I looked back over at Zoe. Her grandfather was also at her table and there was another young lady across from her, also wearing a red dress.

But this girl had lovely brunette hair pulled up messily onto the top of her head.

I instantly thought about Sarah.

Maybe I would slip away from this madness early and go back to her hotel.

Maybe I'd get lucky and find her there.

Thinking about that distracted me from the insanity that had become my family.

Then the girl in the red dress... the girl with her back to me... turned her head so that I could see her profile.

Good God. I was seeing Sarah everywhere.

She wouldn't be at this fundraiser. She had an interview.

With a pharmaceutical company.

Mr. Madris owned a pharmaceutical company.

No. Not possible.

The odds of that happening were far too steep.

I was fairly certain I was staring a hole through whoever that girl was sitting at Mr. Madris's table.

My thoughts were racing about a hundred miles an hour.

If that was Sarah, then I didn't have to go stalk her at her hotel.

If that was Sarah, then I had no idea how I was going to fix this. The woman I was interested in was sitting at the same table with the woman my family wanted me to marry.

If my family honestly thought that, they were certifiably insane and perhaps needed to take some of those psychotropic medications Mr. Madris sold.

23

SARAH

*T*he fundraiser speakers weren't bad, all in all, but I didn't have a lot to compare them to. Keynote conference speakers, maybe.

I sat across from Zoe. She wasn't paying the least bit of attention. She whispered with her two friends throughout the whole thing.

About halfway through the second speaker, I felt like someone was staring at me. But we were sitting two tables back from the speakers, so I dismissed the sensation.

Dinner consisted of a small plate of fish and salad. It tasted a lot better than it looked. Then there was cheesecake.

By then the speakers had finished and it was clear that we were left to our own devices. People would be back to socializing.

I began to plot my exit. Once Mr. Madris was clearly occupied, I could slip out. Unfortunately he seemed intent on introducing both me and Tyler to everyone he knew.

After the cheesecake, I excused myself and made my way to the lady's room. I took my time, using the sitting room to check my messages and just have a moment to relax.

I checked my flight for in the morning. It was still on time and did my electronic check in.

I liked traveling, but I also liked going home. But this time, I felt a vague sense of regret.

It was because of Luke. I rarely let myself entertain being attracted to anyone when I was working.

But I had entertained it with Luke.

It wasn't the smartest thing I'd done lately.

I needed to get back to the table before I was missed. It was too late to dodge out.

I opened the restroom door and stopped dead in my tracks.

Luke was standing across the hallway.

He was wearing a black tux that fit him like it was tailor made.

And he was grinning at me.

"Luke?"

"Of all the places," he said.

"I 'um." I tried to collect my thoughts. I was supposed to have met him at my hotel. "I couldn't get to the hotel. There was an accident on..." whatever that street was. West something.

"I know," he said, holding up an arm.

I put my hand in the crook of his elbow. He smelled like a mixture of vanilla and earthy tones. So deliciously masculine. He'd added a hint of cologne to his clean scent.

"Westheimer," he said. "I saw."

"I didn't purposely stand you up," I said.

"I didn't think so." He steered me away from the tables toward the front doors. "You said you were here for an interview."

"Where are we going?" I asked.

He looked at me with mock surprise. "We have a date, no?"

"Well... yes... but..."

Billionaire's Unexpected Landing　　73

"If you'd rather stay here and endure stuffy conversations," he said, stopping.

"Yeah. No." Absolutely not. "But I need to make an excuse. I'm still kind of sort of on my interview."

"Alright," he said. "Go. Make your excuses. But I'm going to wait out here in the lobby."

I removed my hand from his elbow. "Why are you here anyway?" I asked, stopping halfway through my turn.

"I'll explain later," he said. "It's complicated."

"Complicated. Right." I turned and headed toward my table. In order words he didn't want to talk about it.

That's what complicated usually meant.

Now I had to come with an excuse to get out of here. There was no way I was going to let Luke slip away again.

24

LUKE

I stepped outside into the cool, brisk evening air.

Now all I had to do was to figure how to distract Sarah away from telling her about why I really wanted to get away from here.

My family had gone insane. My father, at least. No one else had said anything to me about the preposterous notion of me marrying Zoe Madris.

People didn't do that anymore.

I took a mint out of my pocket and slipped it into my mouth.

There had to be more to this story than my father was telling me.

Grandpa spent his mornings in his home office so I'd go by his house in the morning and find out if the family was in some kind of financial trouble.

Even if they were, that was no reason for me to marry someone.

I shuddered and bit the mint in half.

Even if I hadn't just met Sarah, I still didn't want to marry someone just for a business deal.

Billionaire's Unexpected Landing

Forcing myself to put that whole thing in the back of my mind, I focused on what Sarah and I could do.

There had to be something we could do that would distract her away from wanting to talk about my family.

Maybe I'd take her for pizza and wine at a little pizzeria I knew. We were a little bit—a lot—overdressed for it, but that could be part of the fun.

I could take her up for a night flight. But she was flying out in the morning so that didn't seem like something she would enjoy right now.

We could go to the opera, but it was too late. It was too late to plan anything really.

Maybe we'd just go to a cocktail bar and talk.

It didn't really matter to me so much what we did. I just wanted to be around her.

It seemed like such a stroke of luck that we'd ended up in the same place on this one night.

My grandma Savannah would call it fate. Just like when she had accidentally run into Grandpa after all those years apart.

I turned at the sound of her heels coming toward me.

She was stunningly beautiful.

She stopped a mere foot in front of me.

"I think you may be getting me in trouble," she said, but there was a glimpse of a smile playing about her lips.

"Not possible," I said.

"Oh, I think it's actually quite possible," she said, looking up toward the sky. "So now that you've sprung me from this place, what are we going to do?"

"What do you want to do?"

"Oh no," she said. "You're the one who's from here."

"Well…" I said. "Are you hungry?"

"Not really. The fish was pretty good."

"You liked the fish?"

"Sure," she said. "didn't you?"

"I don't think you're supposed to like the food at these things."

"It beats what they usually feed me," she said.

I looked at her in a different light. I had the idea that drug reps were wined and dined. I guess I should know better than to believe the myths.

Just like pilots. People had the misperception that being a pilot was a glamourous life. But typically it wasn't. Of course, it didn't hurt that my family owned a fleet of airplanes.

I held up my arm again.

"Let's have a cocktail at a quiet little lounge I know," I said. "Is that okay with you?"

She put her hand on my arm. "Sounds perfect."

25

SARAH

*A*fter a short ride in Luke's red Maserati sports car, we valeted at a cocktail bar not far from my hotel.

He was right. It was relatively quiet. Jazz music playing in the background. Cozy little round booths perfect for couples.

The hostess led him to the one little round booth that happened to be available. I almost got a sense that it had been reserved for him. Almost.

I slid in one side and he slid in on the other and we almost bumped into each other in the middle.

He was smiling at me again.

A server, a young lady, appeared at our table.

"Good evening," she said, pleasantly. "What would you like?"

Luke looked to me. "What would you like?"

"A glass of cabernet, please," I said.

"Make that two," he said.

The young server smiled and dashed off.

Within seconds, she was back with not only two glasses of wine, but two empty wine glasses and a bottle of cabernet.

"We just got this in," she said, setting the glasses on our table. "I think you'll like it."

"Sounds good, Amy," Luke said.

I watched as she deftly removed the cork and poured a taste into one glass and handed it to Luke.

He swirled it, then sipped.

"Nice," he said.

The server, Amy, smiled and filled both our glasses.

"You've been here before," I said, after Amy walked off, leaving the bottle sitting on our table.

"Guilty as charged." He lifted his glass. "To fate," he said.

I tapped my glass against his, then took a sip of the wine. He was right. It was a good wine.

Being from California, I'd tasted a lot of wine.

"You know wine?" he asked.

"A little," I said. "I should know more than I do. My grandfather owned a winery."

"No way," he said, leaning forward. "That is so cool."

"Maybe," I said, with a shrug. "My father sold the winery when I was a baby."

"But… why?" Luke asked.

"My mother got sick and we needed the money for her treatment."

Luke set his glass down. "I am so sorry. How…?" He seemed to stop himself before he asked too much.

I took another sip of the wine. It was a story I had told before. It was almost like the story belonged to someone else.

"She passed away anyway," I said. "when I was five years old."

He leaned forward, looking into my eyes.

"And that's how you got interested in pharmaceuticals," he said.

"I won't say it's not," I said. "but I was only five, so…" I shrugged. "probably."

And somehow I had just bared my soul to a man I barely knew and somehow it didn't feel wrong.

26

LUKE

I wanted to wrap my arms around Sarah and hold her close.

This girl's life had started out with trauma and yet she seemed to have turned out so normal. So perfect.

I'd been around my grandmother and my aunts enough to know just enough about psychology to be dangerous.

I knew that early childhood trauma could affect a person for the rest of their lives, but at the same time, children were resilient. How they dealt with the trauma often depended on the other people in their lives.

"And your father?" I asked, needing to know. Needing to know that she had someone in her life to make up for the losses she had experienced.

"He's a college professor," she said with a little smile. "He teaches music."

"Music?"

"I know," she said. "An odd thing to teach."

"No," I said. "Not odd. Just not what I expected."

"How so?"

"Well." I refilled my wine glass. "Your father seems like a

practical man. Doing what he had to do to help your mother. Yet music isn't practical." I swirled the wine in my glass. "but on the other hand, what he did for her was romantic and music is romantic."

"I never really thought about it that way," she said, looking at me blankly.

"I learned everything I know about human nature from my grandmother," I said.

"And?" she said. "What about flying?"

"Ah." I twirled my wine glass by the stem, watching the swirling deep violet liquid. "I got that love from my grandfather. He had me in an airplane by the time I could toddle."

"You've got such good memories." Her smile held a touch of sadness.

I felt like I had walked into her private territory. But I was there now. There was no going back.

"But you were raised by your father," I said, taking a sip of wine.

"True," she said, running a finger along the edge of her glass. "But he was never the same after that. He became distant."

I waited. Letting the silence stretch, giving her time to collect her thoughts.

"He eventually remarried," she said, keeping her gaze focused on the wine. "When I was fourteen. It was not a good year."

"I'm so sorry you had to go through that," I said, going with my impulse and putting a hand over hers.

"It was a long time ago," she said, looking up at me with a little smile and a shrug. But I could see the pain in her eyes. It wasn't THAT long ago in the great scheme of things.

This conversation had gone to a much darker place that I had intended. This wasn't the kind of thing people like to talk about on first dates.

Billionaire's Unexpected Landing 81

But as I sat there with my hand over hers, I knew that it had gone where I had wanted it to go. I didn't want to know what her favorite color was or where she'd gone to college. Those were surface things that I could learn later. I wanted to know the real Sarah Lawrence.

I looked up then to see Zoe Madris walking through the front door, her two close friends, Beau and Charlie following at her heels.

Panic shot through me. Did she know about the scheme our parents were concocting? If she did, was she on board with it?

And perhaps ever more immediately important, was that why she was here?

"I need a favor," I said, my gaze not leaving Zoe.

"What is it?" Sarah asked as Zoe headed straight for our table. I don't think she saw me yet.

I turned and gazed at Sarah. Zoe was almost to our table.

"It's a favor I'll apologize for up front," I said.

Then I planted my lips on hers.

I had planned on this being a brief kiss. Just enough to make a point. For Zoe to see. But once my lips touched Sarah's, I felt my world tilt on its axis.

Everything I knew about the world shifted. And I didn't want to let her go.

Ever.

Sarah didn't move.

I forgot the motivation behind kissing her.

Or maybe Zoe wasn't the motivation so much as she was the excuse.

I'm not sure how many seconds ticked past. Enough that I knew Zoe had walked past us.

I also knew that she saw us.

I knew because this was my booth and she knew it.

The Compass Lounge was owned by Worthington Enterprises. And I had controlling interest in it.

So although my father did not share Worthington Enterprises financials with me, I knew that *The Compass Lounge* was solid.

When I pulled my lips from hers, the look on her face was one of surprise and something else. Something else that made me want to do it again.

She blinked as though waking up.

"What was that about?" she asked, searching my eyes.

Shifting in my seat, I looked to my left, over to where Zoe and her friends were sitting now.

Zoe met my gaze for a mere instant, before darting away. I couldn't read it. I didn't know her that well. I didn't know her at all. When it came right down to it, I only knew her well enough to recognize her in a crowd. I'd had maybe a couple of brief conversations with her.

"I... 'um..." I was the one who was scattered from this kiss. Wasn't it supposed to be the other way around?

She tilted her head to the side and looked at me curiously.

"Something has come up that I need your help with," I said. "That is if you're willing. It's only temporary." I hope. I was coming up with this stuff off the cuff. In truth, I knew nothing about what the extent of what I was asking her.

"It depends on what it is," she said, her tongue darting out to lick her lower lip.

Okay. Maybe this was backfiring on me. Just a little bit.

Maybe a lot.

"It's one of those complicated things."

"Does that mean you can't tell me then?"

"What? No." I straightened my napkin, looking for order.

"Usually when people say something is complicated, they mean they don't want to talk about it."

I grinned.

I liked this girl more by the minute.

27

SARAH

I was having a bit of trouble following my own thoughts.

They kept straying back to that kiss.

Luke had just kissed me. Out of the blue.

And he had apologized to me before he did it.

It's was the oddest first kiss I had ever had.

And it was the best first kiss I had ever had.

It had been light. But firm.

I had been too stunned to resist.

And I knew in my heart that I would not have resisted anyway.

I'd been imagining this since the moment I'd met him.

Or some rendition of it. I certainly hadn't imagined him apologizing then planting his lips on mine.

And I certainly had not imagined that I would have such a profound response to him.

The electricity I had felt yesterday when I'd put my hand in his, was nothing compared to the bolt of lightning that shot through my system when his lips touched mine.

He said he had an explanation, but it was complicated. He said he would tell me anyway, but he seemed reluctant to do so.

"I think my family—perhaps my father specifically—may be losing touch with reality."

"Why do you say that?" I asked with a little laugh. "He's too old to have a schizophrenic break."

"Is he?" Luke asked, turning to me. He was serious. He was really asking me this question.

"I'm not a psychiatrist," I said, looked at him sideways. He looked quite serious about this.

He ran a hand through his hair and looked at me.

"Never mind," he said. "It's too ridiculous to even talk about."

"I knew this was going to happen," I said, looking away. "I need to find the lady's room."

He pointed to my left. Past Zoe, Mr. Madris's granddaughter, also known as the girl with the platinum hair and her two friends who had just been seated.

It occurred to me in that moment, that Zoe had walked by just as Luke had kissed me.

Without waiting for further response from Luke, I slid out of the booth, adjusted my skirts, and headed to the restroom.

I needed to get away from him for a second. To reclaim my wits. When he had kissed me, my thoughts had scattered like leaves in the wind.

I was already attracted to him. He just made it worse.

I stepped inside the lady's room and sat in one of the two armchairs. This ladies lounge was clean and modern looking with a new look and feel to it.

I checked my lipstick, then sat and took a couple of deep relaxing breaths.

When Luke had said things were complicated, I'd known he wasn't going to explain.

Billionaire's Unexpected Landing 85

But it was okay. I was only here for one night. It was just one date.

Then I was back to California.

I most certainly did not need to get attached to him.

Even if I did get the job here, I still didn't need to get attached to him.

Luke didn't strike me as the kind of guy a girl should get attached to.

He barely knew me and already he'd kissed me. Not exactly a sign that he was a commitment kind of guy.

I reminded myself that I wasn't looking for a relationship either. Especially not what had a high chance of being a long-distance relationship.

Tyler had what could be called the home field advantage. He was already here. Everyone knew him. Knew what they would be getting. There would be no moving costs required.

My competitive side wanted the job, of course, but I liked my job on the west coast.

I enjoyed most of my clients and would miss them. I would also miss spending my days in the field. This role, I'd learned, was more of a supervisory role.

Calmer, now, I stood up to leave. To go back to Luke's booth.

Zoe walked in just as I was reaching for the door.

"Hello Zoe," I said, with a smile.

"Hello," she said with that tight, controlled smile that I recognized as one that high society women used when forced to be polite.

She saw me as beneath her in social status. That frankly meant nothing to me, but to girls like Zoe, it meant everything.

It was how they categorized their world.

I didn't hate her for it. It was how she'd been raised.

Mr. Madris's son would be her father, but she likely learned this from her mother.

Putting her out of my mind, I went back out to continue my date with Luke.

He didn't have to tell me anything he didn't want to tell me.

It was just a date.

Just one date.

Then tomorrow I would be leaving.

28

LUKE

I tensed as Zoe followed Sarah to the lady's room.
Please let it be a coincidence.

I did not want Zoe messing with Sarah. Not in any shape or form.

I'd told myself I didn't care... that it didn't matter if she knew about my father's business proposition. But right now it mattered very much.

Right now I needed to know.

I needed to know what kind of trouble I was looking at.

This was my cocktail lounge.

I had designed it and had it built. I didn't actually build it and didn't claim to. But I'd worked with one of my cousins, an architect, on the design and I was quite proud of it.

It was my first venture project outside of aviation.

Grandpa Noah had taught me to never, ever put all my eggs in one basket. He'd taught me the importance of diversifying.

He'd warned me that anything could happen. I could lose an eye. I could be diagnosed with something like high blood pressure that would keep me from flying.

88   KATHRYN KALEIGH

Always have a backup plan, he'd told me repeatedly.

He hadn't exactly followed his own advice, at least not at first when he was growing Skye Travels, but I guess with age came wisdom. And he passed that wisdom down to me. He'd pass it to my brother as well, but Dylan wasn't ready to hear anything serious.

When I spotted Sarah coming back towards me, all in one piece, I let out a breath I hadn't realized I'd been holding.

She was stunning in her long red dress. Absolutely stunning.

Sitting down, she slid around the circle booth to sit next to me again.

"Did you miss me?" she asked, flirtatiously.

"Without a doubt," I said.

She grinned. "Good. Because you have a complicated story to tell me."

I didn't know what one had to do with the other, but I'd learned a long time ago that following female logic was not something a sane man would attempt.

"Are you sure?" I asked. "Because I'd much rather talk about you."

"Nice try," she said, lifting her glass in my direction. "But I'm not falling for that one."

"Okay," I said with a shrug. "But don't say I didn't warn you."

"Deal," she said.

"Alright," I said, sitting back and preparing myself. I said I'd tell her and I owed it to her now that I had kissed her in the name of saving myself from Zoe.

I decided to jump right in and start in the middle.

"My father has decided that I need to marry."

"*Need* to marry?" she asked, looking as perplexed about it as I felt.

Billionaire's Unexpected Landing 89

"Yes."

"Like in the 1700s kind of need to marry?"

"I suppose so," I said. "since he has picked out the girl." I held up a finger, getting warmed up to the subject. "And he's calling it a business merger."

29

SARAH

This is worse than I had expected.

Luke's father wanted him to marry for convenience.

"Is that even a thing?" I asked. "Anymore?"

"I don't really know," Luke said. "Apparently my father thinks it is."

"What are you going to do?"

He looked at me a bit stunned.

"What am I supposed to do?" he asked.

"Do you love her?" I asked. This was a conversation I had never had with anyone and I'd had some pretty bizarre conversations over the years.

"What?" He made a face. "No. I don't even know her. I mean I know her, but I've talked to you more than I've ever talked to her."

"Well," I said. "That is a bit peculiar."

When Amy dropped off some pretzels Luke picked one up and bit off the end.

"I'm actually wondering if I should take my father in for a psychological evaluation," he said.

Billionaire's Unexpected Landing 91

I laughed. That was not what I expected him to say. And oddly enough, it made me feel better. The thought that he would consider an arranged marriage made our date seem pointless and me feel like a fool.

"Did you ask your mother about it?"

"Not yet." He looked toward the bathroom as Zoe came out and sat at her booth with her two friends.

"Don't you think you should?" I asked.

He turned back to me.

"That's her," he said.

"Who's her?" I asked, confused. "Your mother?"

"No," he said, nodding back toward Zoe. "That's her. Zoe."

"Mr. Madris's granddaughter?"

"Yes."

"What about her?"

"My father wants me to marry her," he said. "Zoe."

"That's so…" I didn't know what to say. Weird. Insane.

"Exactly," he said.

"I interviewed with her grandfather. Clinical Pharm."

"I sort of figured that out. That makes it even more strange."

I ran a fingertip around the edge of the glass. Maybe it was a small world I was walking into. Obviously Mr. Madris would be a wealthy man and obviously the Worthingtons would be in the same orbit.

In that case, it was a little bit less strange that they all knew each other. Not less strange that Luke's father was attempting to have Luke marry Mr. Madris's granddaughter. On a business arrangement.

The whole thing made my head spin.

But he seemed to be genuinely asking for my help.

"When did you find this out?" I asked, trying to focus. I wasn't a psychiatrist or a psychologist, but because I knew psychotropic drugs, people tended to think I had the skills to help them.

"Just tonight," he said. "Before the fundraiser."

"Oh. Wow. That's bad timing." I didn't know what I meant by that exactly. Bad timing for him in general or bad timing for our date. Maybe all of it.

"I can't think of a time that would be good," he said.

I looked over at Zoe. At her two boyfriends, one on either side.

"Does she know about it?" I asked, looking back at Luke.

He shook his head.

"I don't know yet." The music changed keys. Went from upbeat to a more somber note.

"At any rate," he said. "Thank you for helping me."

I don't think I've done anything," I said.

He grinned and lifted his glass. "We'll see, won't we?"

30

LUKE

I was still disturbed by the whole thing with Zoe, but talking to Sarah made me feel somewhat better.

Grandma always insisted that it helped to talk about things.

I honestly had not had that many problems in my life up until now.

I'd never been as carefree as my brother, but I hadn't carried the weight of the world on my shoulders either.

The music was far too somber. I thought about going to the back and changing the song, but I wasn't ready to tell Sarah that this was my cocktail lounge.

She already knew things about me that no one else knew.

Even though I had joked about having Father evaluated, I didn't believe that was the problem.

I didn't know what exactly the problem was. Not yet.

But after I caught Grandpa in the morning, I would have a better idea.

I could see Zoe out of the corner of my eye. Her gaze kept straying in our direction.

She had never given me the time of day before and I hadn't cared.

She had more boyfriends than any girl could possibly need. In fact, right now, she had two of her boyfriends with her.

As far as I could tell, they didn't mind that they were one of many.

I wasn't attracted to that kind of girl. When I had a girlfriend, I wanted her all to myself.

It was just the way I was built.

At any rate, I decided that she had to know about the business deal, also known as the marriage. It was the only thing that would explain why she kept glancing in this direction.

The whole idea made me sick to my stomach.

Here I was with a beautiful woman that I enjoyed talking to… that I was attracted to…that kissing had felt like walking inside a rainbow… and here we were talking about Zoe.

Zoe was a situation that would sort itself out.

I'd make sure of that. I'd find out what exactly what was going on with my family and I would take that whole marriage thing off the table.

With renewed determination, I turned to Sarah.

"Enough about me," I said. "Tell me something about you I don't know."

"That would be just about anything, wouldn't it?" she asked on a bubble of laughter.

I grinned. "I suppose. But I do know some things about you."

She took a sip of her wine and looked at me from beneath her lashes in what could only be described as a flirtatious look. My stomach flipped upside down.

"And what things would that be?" she asked, batting her lashes.

I sat back and cleared my throat. I was feeling a bit tight all the way to my core.

"I know that you are a pharmaceutical sales representative from Los Angeles interviewing for a job in Houston," I said.

Billionaire's Unexpected Landing   95

"How do you know I'm from Los Angeles?"

"I looked up your flight," I said, with a little shrug. "And I found your information." I wouldn't apologize for it. I had to know things about my passengers.

"Okay. That's basic," she said. "What else do you have?"

"I know that you're kind and responsible."

"True." She picked up a pretzel and took a little nibble.

Watching her lips had me thinking things I most definitely should not be thinking about.

I struggled to rein my thoughts back in.

"But you're right," I said. "There are so many things I don't know. Things I would like to know." I added with a lift of one eyebrow.

She smiled. Then as something I couldn't read shifted in her gaze, she fisted a hand in my shirt and pulling me close, kissed me.

31

SARAH

*L*uke wanted me to help him, so I was going to help him.

Zoe was walking this way and from her expression, she had something to say to Luke.

Since he wanted me to help him avoid marrying her, I had to help him. That was, at least, my intent when I pulled him close for a kiss.

But now that my lips were pressed against his, I was pretty sure that Zoe was merely an excuse to kiss him again.

After a few seconds, I loosened my hold on his shirt and leaned back just enough that I could look into his eyes. Clear sapphire with little flakes of silver.

Oh my.

This had so backfired on me.

He was looking at me as though he wanted to do far more things than kiss me. Maybe even right here. Right now.

But then Zoe cleared her throat and we both looked at her. She was a striking young woman, tall and slim, wearing a turquoise mermaid dress that accented her perfectly coifed blonde hair with hints of auburn streaks.

Billionaire's Unexpected Landing 97

She was standing there, her arms crossed, her blonde hair falling around her shoulders, looking like a very vexed goddess.

I released Luke's shirt and, smoothing his shirt a little, straightened in my seat.

I looked at her and blinked, enjoying the lingering feel of Luke's lips against mine while trying to keep my expression blank as I looked at Zoe.

"Hello, Zoe," Luke said. "How are you?" He sounded so incredibly calm.

"I'm good. Thank you for asking." Zoe's tone was crisp and to the point.

Then there was silence. One of Zoe's boyfriends came up and stood next to her in what looked like a show of solidarity.

"What's up, Zoe?" Luke asked, with an enviable casualness.

Zoe's gaze flicked from him to me and back again.

"We need to talk," she said.

Although Luke's expression didn't change, I felt the tension radiating off him.

"Sure," he said, with a shrug. "Call Skye Travels tomorrow and schedule an appointment."

He was good. I had to give him that. Very impressive. Keep business as business.

Even if it was a marriage.

Zoe was looking vexed again.

"It's not business." Her gaze flicked to mine again. "Exactly."

Luke lifted an eyebrow. "If it's social, you can have a seat and we'll talk about it right now."

Vexed. Most definitely vexed.

"No," she said. "I'll make the appointment." Then she turned and walk away, her friend behind her. The little sway of her hips looked as natural as breathing.

Luke let out a breath.

"She knows," he said.

"You're right," I said. "And she's not happy."

Luke looked into my eyes and again I was drawn to just how blue his were. Like sapphire orbs.

"But," he said. "Is she not happy about the marriage or is she not happy about… you?"

32

LUKE

*Z*oe was not happy. Anybody could see that.

Surely she didn't want to actually marry me.

And surely she wasn't jealous of Sarah.

Since she and I had never had a conversation of any substance, I could think of no other reason why she would want to talk to me.

None.

My phone chimed with a text. I pulled it out of my jacket pocket to see who was messaging me. It was my younger sister. My only sister, Camila.

Out of five children, my parents had four boys and one girl.

CAMILA: *What have you done?*

I stared at the phone.

"Everything okay?" Sarah asked, seeing my confused expression.

"It's my sister," I said.

ME: *What do you mean?*

CAMILA: *You've upset Zoe.*

I had forgotten that Camila and Zoe were friends. I did not

understand it. How my sister could be friends with a girl like Zoe.

I'd never actually seen the two of them doing anything together. I think they communicated simply because they had gone to high school together. Neither one of them had girlfriends. Zoe had her circle of men and Camila, a pilot, was friends with a lot of guys, but in a different way. A work way.

So I guess since they had a lot of overlap in their friends… a lot of mutual friends, they had somehow become as close to being girlfriends as either of them could tolerate.

ME: *I did not.*

We were talking like we were teenagers again. Sarah was watching me. Waiting.

ME: *Father did it.* I typed in the words. Considered deleting them for about half a second, then hit send.

Father *had* done it. And since Camila and I were close, and she was close to father, let her take it up with him.

I put my phone on silent and tucked it back in my pocket.

"She…" I caught myself. I did not want to spend my entire evening with Sarah talking about another woman. One who meant nothing to me.

Sarah raised an eyebrow and looked at me. I changed course.

"I believe we were talking about you."

She sat back, the flirtatiousness evaporating from her demeanor.

"Let's not ruin a perfectly good evening," she said.

Sarah was the most perplexing female I had ever met. Most women wanted to talk about themselves at every opportunity.

"Then what do you suggest we talk about?"

"Who says we have to talk?" she asked.

My mind automatically went south and my throat went dry.

"No one," I said.

Billionaire's Unexpected Landing 101

Smiling again, she pulled out her phone and a couple of minutes later, she held it up for me to see.

"Is this a place we can go?" she asked.

"Seriously?" I asked, looking at her screen.

She shrugged.

I thought for moment, then grinned. "I can do better than that."

33

SARAH

"Who lives here?" I asked as we pulled into the high rise circle drive.

Three valets immediately stepped up. One opened Luke's door, one opened mine, and another held the door to the building open.

"Good evening, Luke," one said as Luke handed him the keys.

"How are you, Miss?" The second valet held my door open.

"Good," I said. "Thank you."

Luke was at my door before I had time to straighten.

"I've got it," he said, crowding out my valet.

Luke held out a hand and I gratefully accepted his help. There was something unexpectedly strange and yet comforting about his little show of possessiveness.

The third valet held the door open as Luke and I walked into a huge, oversized lobby with a concierge about fifty yards across the marble-floored room with mile high ceilings. Although there was room for about a hundred people to move about easily, we were the only ones other than staff here.

We turned right and walked straight to an elevator.

Billionaire's Unexpected Landing　　103

Luke pulled a key fob from his pocket and pressed the button.

"No one right now," Luke said, finally answering my question.

The elevator door opened and we stepped inside.

He pressed what looked like a combination of buttons.

"But this is your property?" I asked, noting the key fob in his hand.

"It's an investment property," he said. "But no one's using it right now."

"I see." Though I didn't.

I had asked Luke to take me to a pool hall, but he insisted that we were far too overdressed for that.

Said he had a better idea.

As I watched the elevator buttons clicking off the numbers, I considered the possibilities.

My first thought was that Luke had friends who lived here, but he said it was an investment property.

There was a big difference between an investment property in a high rise condo and a pool hall.

"I can get a chaperone if you'd like," he said, with just a hint of a smile playing about his lips.

"I don't think that will be necessary," I said as the elevator doors opened on the twenty-ninth floor, but the thought of being alone with Luke had my breath hitching.

We stepped directly from the elevator into the condo. As Luke flipped on lights, I walked across to the wall of windows overlooking the city of Houston.

Downtown looked like no more than a little cluster of buildings from here. I had a nice enough condo, but it was on the third floor. And I had to walk down a hallway to go inside.

It did not hold a candle to this place.

I couldn't even imagine what it might be like to live on the twenty-ninth floor with a view like this.

"Beautiful," I said as Luke came to stand next to me.

"One of the best in the city."

I had no reference point, but I couldn't disagree with him.

"You ready?" he asked.

"Sure."

I followed him around to the north side of the condo into what looked like a game room with equally magnificent views.

"How's this?" he asked, handing me a pool stick.

"Very private." I laughed, taking the pool stick from him.

"Would you like a cold beer?" he asked. "I have a flight in the morning, so I can't have anything else. Minimum twelve hours bottle to throttle."

"You must have a late flight," I said, drawn to the view again. "No beer for me either," I added over my shoulder.

"Do you want to break?" he asked.

She turned around and grinned. "Nah. You go ahead."

"Suit yourself."

34

LUKE

*T*he way the balls slammed into each other as they landed in the pockets, resembled the sounds of a pool hall.

I had gotten one ball in on my break and that had been lucky.

Sarah was currently on her fifth shot without missing. After the first ball smacked into the side pocket, she'd kicked off her heels.

I'd often thought about moving into this condo and it still wasn't out of the question.

This property was an investment property I'd bought with Grandpa's guidance.

He and I had stood right here looking out at this view and decided that we were going to make this a fun place to live.

A wet bar and a pool table to go with the private pool. The rest of the furnishings—it was fully furnished—came from Grandma's guidance. Needless to say, it was tastefully furnished, befitting the elegance of the building itself. Between the two of them, I had learned a lot over that summer just after I graduated college.

It was part of my grandfather's hands on training that a man should never put all his eggs in one basket.

And the choices we'd made, the things they had taught me, held some of my fondest memories of them.

Other than that, I'd never spent time here with anyone other than my siblings.

Having Sarah here—enjoying it—made me proud of what Grandpa and I had put together from our vision that started with a pool table.

And right now, looking back, this was my explanation for why I'd been dragging my feet on leasing it out. It had just gotten a new reason for being vacant.

Sarah slammed another ball into a corner pocket.

"I think that was a trick shot," I told her.

"What's a trick shot?" she asked on a bubble of laughter, standing her cue stick straight up.

"You know what a trick shot is," I said.

She shrugged and picked up her pool cue. How was it that she looked so damned sexy wearing a cocktail dress, barefoot, and holding a cue stick?

"You're just miffed because I'm running the table," she said, leaning over for her next shot.

"Well," I said, pretending to give this a lot of thought. "I think we need to start calling our shots."

"You can't change the rules in the middle of the game." She lowered her cue stick. "Five ball in the side pocket," she said.

When the five ball landed in the side pocket, she smiled gleefully.

"Now you're just showing out," I said.

"Maybe a little." She made a face, but it did not hide her obvious happiness.

"A little my ass," I said.

"Go ahead," she said. "You can take a turn."

"Oh no," I said. "You aren't going to throw the game on my

Billionaire's Unexpected Landing 107

account." Leaning on my cue stick, I nodded toward the table. "Please. I want to watch."

Lowering her gaze, she looked away, but then she shrugged and made the next shot.

"Where did you learn to play?" I asked.

"You're just trying to distract me," she said, walking around the table looking for her next shot. I didn't see one, but hell, maybe she did.

"A common tactic," I said. "But I really want to know."

"Okay," she said after the satisfactory thunk of another ball into the side pocket. "My grandfather, the other one, actually had a pool table in his house. I spent a lot of time there after my mother..."

She trailed off and bent over for the next shot.

I was learning so much about her. The problem was the more I learned, the more I wanted to know.

35

SARAH

I was good at pool. Very good. I considered it one of my hidden super powers.

Glancing over at Luke, handsome and debonair in his tux, I wondered what his super power was. Maybe it his ability to increase the heart rate of women around him.

A heartthrob. I laughed silently at myself. Now I understood where that word came from.

I hadn't planned on running the game. Actually, I couldn't remember the last time I'd even tried.

It wasn't even the satisfying thunk of the balls landing in the pockets or the little shot of dopamine that came with each success.

It was the way Luke was watching me.

When he said he was enjoying watching me, all sorts of things—inappropriate things—came to mind.

So I focused on the game.

And let him watch.

It was so quiet up here. Only the distant roar of a loud muffler now and then. But up here on the twenty-ninth floor, there was just peace and quiet.

Billionaire's Unexpected Landing   109

Luke pulled two water bottles from a little refrigerator and handed one to me.

Besides the pool table in the middle of the room and the swimming pool just outside, the game room had a full wet bar. There was a small sofa on one side of the room and a little bistro table with two chairs in front of the glass window.

There was only one large abstract pastel painting and it was on the wall behind the sofa.

The water was cool and fresh and helped to calm some of the tension I felt just from being around Luke.

It was good tension, but tension nonetheless.

"Are you sure you don't want to take a turn?" I asked, feeling a little bit guilty at hogging the game.

He leaned back against the wall in a perfect display of charming and confident maleness.

"I'd actually like to see you make a perfect game," he said "I've never seen anyone do that before."

I rolled my hands along the cue stick, feeling a bit more pressure now to not miss.

"Have you ever done it?" he asked. "Made a perfect game?"

"I've done it twice," I said. "And both times I was alone at my grandfather's house." I leaned over and aimed. "So I have no witnesses."

The ball went into the side pocket.

"This time you'll have a witness," he said.

I grinned. "That would be nice. Though at the moment..." I walked around the table. "I'm not seeing a clear shot."

"Ah," he said, lifting his water bottle. "I have a good feeling you'll figure something out."

"Well, I have to now, don't I?" I said, looking at him from beneath my lashes.

"No pressure," he said, holding up a hand. "Just a prediction."

"Alright," I said. "No pressure." I lined up what looked like an impossible shot and went for it.

"Besides, I rather like a challenge."

But the ball edged to the side of the table and hovered near the pocket. It wasn't going to make it.

"Well," I said, turning to him. "That was fun while it lasted."

Then I heard the crack of the ball as it landed in the pocket with the other balls.

"It did not go in," I said, looking at Luke.

"Oh. It did." He grinned. "Can you make three more? And then you'll have your third perfect game. And this time with a witness."

I finished off my water and dropped it in the wastebasket at the wet bar on the far side of the room.

When I'd asked to go to a pool hall, it was really just to give us something to do besides talk about Zoe.

I had envisioned a loud bar with loud music. One where it was hard to hear each other talk.

But here we were ensconced in perfect privacy twenty-nine stories in the air.

There was no one around to distract us from each other. It was one of those oddly intimate places for two people to spend time together, especially a couple who had been dating for awhile. When they just wanted some alone time.

So this was completely unexpected, yet at the same time, it was exhilarating.

I squared my shoulders. I'd come too far to throw the game now.

I really had no choice but to keep going.

He was right. If I did manage a perfect game—my third—I would have a witness.

That was motivation enough for me to keep going.

As the last ball landed in the side pocket, it occurred to me

Billionaire's Unexpected Landing

that my grandfather would have been incredibly proud of me right now.

I'd just done something not many people could do.

Turning, I grinned at him.

"You should play professionally," Luke said.

36

LUKE

Sarah looked like the goddess of billiards, standing there in her red cocktail dress, her face flushed, holding the cue stick in one hand like a staff.

The sound of the last ball crashing against the others in a side pocket lingered in the air, then it was quiet.

The air conditioner kicked on, adding a steady background roar.

I took a step forward.

"I'm very impressed," I said. "and honored to be your witness."

She laughed.

"I didn't set out to do that."

"I know you didn't," I said, taking another step toward her. "And that makes it all the sweeter."

Something flicked in her eyes. Awareness.

Her knuckles were white from clutching the cue stick and her lips parted a little.

As I took another step forward, she licked her lips. I stood about three feet in front of her now.

Billionaire's Unexpected Landing 113

"There's no one here," she said, her voice a bit breathy. "No one who needs to be... misled."

"There are some things that don't require a witness." I smiled as I took another step closer.

Her breath hitched just a little and the smile slowly faded from her lips.

I could see the green in her eyes now. Emerald green with little shards of jade giving them even more depth.

I'd always had a weakness for girls with green eyes. Ever since first grade when I'd been enchanted with little Mary Beth Tobias.

She'd had unforgettable green eyes a lot like Sarah's. I'd been spellbound.

But, of course, I'd been in first grade so any chance of stealing a kiss was beyond my scope.

But Sarah. This was a whole different world. And since I'd already tasted those lips of hers... lips that tasted like honey, no one could blame me for wanting more.

My gaze never leaving hers, I took the cue stick from her hand and laid it on the pool table.

Now she had no imaginary shield between us.

I took her hands gently in mine and brought one, then the other up to lightly kiss the back of her fingers.

"The hands of a pool goddess." I turned them over, palm up.

She smiled again as was my intention.

It was enough of an invitation for me to pull her into my arms.

She fit perfectly in my arms, her head resting just beneath my chin.

I felt her sigh and wondered what that meant.

I shifted back just enough to put one hand beneath her chin, tilting her face to mine.

Her eyes were closed as I moved in and kissed her.

As she'd pointed out, there were no witnesses, so I felt no pressure to rush through savoring the feel of our lips together.

But she wrapped her arms around me and leaned in, obviously asking for more.

And being the gentleman that I was, I obliged. Her lips parted enough that our tongues found each other. Hers was velvety soft against mine.

This condo was completely furnished and with other women I would have taken advantage of the king bed in the master bedroom two doors down.

But being the gentleman that I was, I was not going to take advantage of that. That wasn't why I had brought her here. I had brought her to play pool and to just spend more time with her.

But a saint I was not.

37

SARAH

I fell into Luke's kiss and didn't care to ever come out. His lips were that perfect mix of gentle and firm and the more we kissed, the more we couldn't stop.

One of his hands supported my back and the other splayed across my cheek, tangling in my hair.

His lips never leaving mine, he reached down, lifted me up into his arms, and carried me to the little sofa on one side of the room.

Sitting down, with me in his lap now, his lips continue to explore and taste mine.

His tongue swept up and explored the roof of my mouth, something so intimate that it nearly took my breath away.

A clock in one of the other rooms began to chime the hour.

It chimed ten times.

"Don't you—" I could barely speak between kisses. "Have a flight…?"

"I'll cancel," he said.

Something inside me soared, even if only for a moment before I remembered.

"I have a flight…" I said. "Morning,"

"Cancel," he murmured against my lips before he deepened the kiss again.

I forgot to worry as his lips claimed mine.

Then my work ethic creeped back into my consciousness and demanded attention.

"I have—"

He rained kisses across my cheek toward my ear and I forgot what I was going to say as tingles shot through my system.

"What do you have, love?" he asked.

No thoughts.

"I 'um…'" What did I have?

Did he just call me love?

I was getting in over my head.

"Appointments," I said, my thoughts pushing back to the surface.

"Tomorrow?" His lips met mine again briefly then he kissed his way to my other ear.

Oh. My. All my nerve endings gathered in my core, taking all my thoughts with them.

His lips made their way back to mine and my arms wound around his neck. My fingers lightly tugging at the soft hair that stopped before reaching the top of his collar.

Time and space ceased to exist. Seconds coiled into minutes and minutes into eternity.

He sucked my bottom lip, then pulled back.

No. Don't stop.

I didn't want to ever stop kissing him.

"Do you have appointments tomorrow?" he asked.

"What?" I forced my eyes open enough to see that he was smiling at me.

"Do you have appointments tomorrow?"

How was he able to think coherent thoughts?

"Yeah. No," I said, forcing myself to think. "The next day."

Billionaire's Unexpected Landing

"Then have brunch with me," he said, adjusting me on his lap.

Not smart. This was not smart.

I was shaking my head.

"Okay." It wasn't my fault. I had no control.

He kissed the tip of my nose, then stood up, bringing me with him. My legs were almost too weak to hold me.

This man had that effect on me.

"I'll drive you to your hotel," he said, taking my hand.

38

LUKE

*A*n hour later, I stood with Sarah outside her hotel door.

"Where's your cell?" I asked.

She reached into the little handbag hanging from her shoulder and took out her cell and her door key.

When I held out my hand, she placed her phone in mine.

With a little smile, I held it in front of her face to unlock it.

I added my name and phone number as one of her contacts, put it in her favorites, then sent myself a message. My phone chimed once in my pocket.

She watched me quizzically until I handed it back to her.

Pulling her into my arms, I kissed her again before resolutely pulling away.

She had me under her spell and I couldn't get enough of her.

Then she smiled, lightly pressed a finger against my lips, and used her key card to unlock the door.

"Good night," she said, going inside and closing the door behind her.

I stood there, staring at the closed door.

Billionaire's Unexpected Landing 119

I hadn't expected to go inside. Hadn't planned on it.

But now that there was a door between us, I missed her already.

I took out my cell phone and typed a message to her.

ME: *I miss you already.*

Then I put my phone back in my pocket and made my way downstairs to my car.

We hadn't set a time to meet tomorrow, but I would text her in the morning.

I needed to get home. Get some sleep. I had a lot to do tomorrow.

The first thing I had to do was to get someone to cover my flight. Then I needed to schedule an afternoon flight for two to L.A.

I whistled to myself as I waited for the valet to bring my car around. Knowing I would get to spend most of tomorrow with Sarah brightened my night.

Before I pulled out onto the freeway, waiting for the light to change, I checked my phone for messages.

But there were none.

My brief moment of disappointment was overshadowed by the memory of her lips against mine. She probably turned her phone off at night.

As I pulled into my own garage, I remembered the whole situation with Zoe.

It was funny how I had completely put it out of my mind while I was with Sarah.

I did not have a solution to that other than just flat out saying no, but after I met with Grandpa in the morning, he would know about what was going on.

I was counting on it.

After I got ready for bed, I checked my messages one more time and got a little shot of dopamine when I saw that I had one message.

I quickly opened it up.

Then my spirits plummeted.

UNKNOWN: *Luke. This is Zoe. Can we talk tomorrow?*

With a frustrated groan I turned the phone on silent and set it on the charger.

Hadn't I told her to call the office to make an appointment?

Where had she gotten my number? My sister, no doubt. And it was late, wasn't it?

Just after eleven. Good God. I may be turning into an old man, but I had things to do in the morning.

So Zoe would just have to wait.

39

SARAH

*M*y day started out frantic. Last night had been like a fairy tale, but today was back to normal. Well, maybe not normal, exactly. Again. Frantic.

I woke with two messages on my phone.

The first one made me smile.

LUKE: *I miss you already.*

The second one not so much.

ZACHARY: *I need to meet with you as soon as you get back.*

ZACHARY: *I've scheduled a dinner with Dr. Carlton.*

I dropped the phone onto the bed and drank from the bottle of water on my nightstand.

I was scheduled to fly back to L.A. this morning. Zachary had every right to expect me to be available at dinner, especially a late dinner.

What Zachary did not expect was for me skip my flight back to L.A. so I could hang out with Luke—a man I'd only just met less than two days ago. That would be so irresponsible of me.

I set the empty water bottle aside and pressed my fingers to my swollen lips. I could not remember the last time—if ever—I had been so thoroughly kissed.

Although Luke had not said it straight out, I think he wanted me to skip my flight. That either meant I should reschedule for a later time or... it meant he was going to fly me back to L.A. himself.

He hadn't said that, though.

I dragged myself off the bed and padded into the bathroom.

I was being fanciful.

I had to go by what he had actually said.

And he had not actually said anything. Things tended to get distorted in the haze of kissing.

My flight was scheduled to leave at nine o'clock. It was six thirty-seven. That gave me just enough time to get my shower, get dressed and packed, and make my way to the airport.

Sorry Luke, I thought as I brushed my teeth. We'll have to skip brunch today.

The decision, which I really had no choice about, made me sad. I set the toothbrush down and looked at myself in the mirror.

There was a glow to my skin that hadn't been there in a long time. My lips were just a little puffy with a secret smile and my eyes were brighter.

I thought about what I should text back to Luke. His message had come in last night. Right after he'd dropped me off here. I'd had my phone off so I had not seen it.

I decided not to say anything right now.

I'd figure it out later.

Rushing to get ready, I got dressed and headed downstairs for coffee.

I argued with myself the whole time.

I could tell Zachary that my flight was delayed, but he would know better. I could tell him I got a better offer. But I knew better. How was I supposed to move up the corporate ladder if I didn't bother to show up for important clients? Zachary was not interested in my dating life.

We had an understanding that my dating life came second to my job. Actually it was more like his understanding and my acceptance.

Without anyone interesting to date, I had just let the expectation ride.

Maybe it was about time to do something about it.

40

LUKE

*E*arly the next morning, I pulled into the Skyhouse parking lot. The Skyhouse, across from the Skye Travels terminal was what used to be a bar—unrelated to Skye Travels Airline—and was still a bar, but they had added both breakfast and lunch to their menus.

The scent of coffee and bacon and hashbrowns greeted me as I stepped inside. I'd had one cup of Starbuck's coffee on the drive out to the airport, but there was no such thing as too much coffee.

I had planned on having my first meal of the day with Sarah. Well, that wasn't happening.

The Skyhouse was on the way from River Oaks where I lived to the Woodlands where Grandpa lived so I'd agreed to meet Zoe here for breakfast.

She'd seemed a bit distressed, if I read her texts correctly and I wasn't the kind of man who left a woman in distress. Not even a woman I was expected to marry. A woman I was most definitely NOT going to marry.

Zoe was already sitting at a table, looking quite calm and collected. She was wearing blue jeans and a sweatshirt and her hair streamed over her shoulders. She was really quite beautiful. I had just never been attracted to her.

She watched me as I came in her direction and sat down across from her. She had what looked like an untouched cup of coffee sitting on the table in front of her beside a menu she probably had not touched either.

"Good morning, Zoe," I said, hoping to avoid a confrontation.

"I won't marry you," she said, without any kind of preamble. So no small talk.

All sorts of emotions swirled through me. Confusion. Relief. A little bit of illogical disappointment which I easily dismissed.

No man wanted a girl to tell him she wouldn't marry him. Even if she was a girl he wouldn't marry. And even if he had not asked.

"I think you have me at a disadvantage," I said.

She laced her hands together and leaned forward against the edge of the table.

"You don't know," she said, flatly.

"All I know is what my father told me." I said with a quick shake of my head. "Actually very little."

She sat back and looked away, tears in her eyes.

"Zoe," I said. "My father didn't tell me why. I'm on my way to my grandfather's house now to find out more. But… if you can tell me."

"Something's happened," she said.

"What?"

"Something very bad." She lowered her gaze and wiped the tears that escaped her eyes.

"Zoe."

She turned her gaze back to mine and shook her head.

"I can't tell you," she said, her words barely audible.

I looked around, then although no one was listening, I lowered my voice to a whisper.

"Zoe," I said. "If you don't tell me, how can I know what the reason behind this is? How can I help you?" I waited a beat. "You said you wanted to see me."

"You can't help me," she said. "I shouldn't have come here."

The server, a woman named Mel, stopped at our table.

"Can I get you anything?" she asked, then got a look at Zoe's face. "I'll just come back."

"Thank you," I mouthed, then turned my attention back to Zoe. "Please. Tell me what's happened. Maybe I can help." As long as it doesn't involve marriage.

She made a sound. I couldn't tell if it was a laugh or a sob.

"No one can help me." Then she stood up and dashed out of the restaurant.

41

SARAH

I sat next to the window and watched luggage being unloaded from the large jet as exhausted looking passengers filed off the plane.

According to the loud announcement, we would be boarding on time.

It was a quick turnaround for the airplane and crew.

I took one more sip of my latte before tossing it in the nearest wastebasket. It was getting cold and besides, I needed to drink water to keep from getting dehydrated on the flight.

Sitting back in my seat with my computer bag on the chair next to me, I looked at my phone again.

My message to Luke sat there. Exposed.

ME: *What time is brunch?*

I couldn't tell if it was delivered or not. It didn't say.

I'd composed about ten different follow up messages, but deleted all of them.

I already had one message out there. It would only make me look desperate to add another to it. Then there would be two messages sitting there unanswered. Making me look desperate.

So since I had no response, I went about my business.

I got to the airport. Checked in. And, I confess, I looked over my shoulder constantly. Watching for any sign of a handsome pilot named Luke Worthington.

Even once I was past the check point and even knowing that he wasn't supposed to get past security, I watched for him. I didn't know much about private pilots, but it made sense that he would have access to the airport.

But there was no sign of him.

He wasn't coming.

I swiped out of my messages, checked my email, and resolved not to look at my messages anymore. It was too late anyway. I was moments away from boarding.

I watched a woman wrangle her two children under control while her husband scrolled on his phone. I would not want to be in her position.

"First Class Boarding Now." The clipped voice of the flight attendant getting everyone's attention.

My resolve lasted about five minutes.

Walking toward the gate, I looked at my messages one more time.

Nothing.

It was hard not to think about Luke when I could still feel his lips on mine.

As I settled into my seat, I reminded myself that this was why did not date anyone remotely involved with work. In a weird roundabout way, Luke had something to do with work.

His family wanted him to marry the granddaughter of the man I'd interviewed with.

Geez.

There was no way I was getting this job now.

Zoe would tell her grandfather that she'd seen me kissing Luke and he would decide my character wasn't right for the job.

Billionaire's Unexpected Landing   129

I leaned my head back against the seat and mentally beat myself up.

In my defense, I hadn't known all these interwoven details when he'd asked for help and pressed his lips against him.

"Can I get you a glass of wine?" the flight attendant asked cheerily.

I shook my head and tried to smile. I couldn't even relax my nerves with a glass of wine. As soon as the plane landed, I had to put on my game face and be on my way to the restaurant to meet with Zachary and his important client.

42

LUKE

I was still sitting at the Skyhouse, baffled by my meeting with Zoe, when I got the message from my father.

FATHER: *Had to cancel your flight.*

I somehow kept a straight face while I wanted to shout with glee.

FATHER: *I need you to go to Denver to pick up your aunt.*

And everything crashed back to the ground.

ME: *Madison?*

FATHER: *Yes.*

I'd ordered a cup of coffee and then on second thought had ordered breakfast. I was starving after all.

ME: *Can't Kade bring her?*

Even as I typed the message I knew perfectly well that Kade was in Florida going through a week long pilot training program. I'd almost gone myself.

Bubbles popped up as Father typed something, then disappeared. I could only imagine what he might be typing.

When the server brought my food, I set my phone down on the table and spread butter across a piece of toast.

Billionaire's Unexpected Landing 131

Bubbles appeared again, then disappeared.

If it had been anyone other than my father, it might have been comical. But Father's sense of humor was limited.

I added a swatch of strawberry jelly to the toast and took a bite.

FATHER: *Where are you?*

That was an unexpected question.

ME: *The Skyhouse.*

More bubbles. I finished the toast and moved on to the omelet.

FATHER: *When you finish breakfast, come across to the office.*

I looked around. Did Father have spies? But no one seemed to be paying me the least bit of attention. Except maybe the server, but she was focused on dropping off my check.

ME: *On my way to Grandpa's.*

FATHER: *Come by here first.*

FATHER: *Grandpa will be here when you get back.*

I shrugged. Fine. Father may not ask nicely—with ask being a strong word, but he knew how to run Skye Travels. If he needed me to fly to Denver to pick up my aunt—his sister, then that's what I would do.

As I finished breakfast, I noticed a message from Sarah that I had not seen. She wasn't in my favorites, so I hadn't gotten an alert. I fixed that immediately.

SARAH: *What time is brunch?*

Damn.

I had missed this text from Sarah. Over two hours ago. I'd been driving. Then I'd gotten tied up with Zoe.

I checked the time. It was too late for brunch.

Sarah's plane would be leaving now. And I needed to take a flight to Denver.

I have screwed this one up good.

I hoped she had not been waiting on me and missed her

flight. If she had, I would have to talk to Father. Figure something out.

There was only one way to find out.

ME: *Where are you?*

I rolled my eyes at myself. There was no denying that I was my father's son.

Unlike last night, the message didn't say delivered.

Sitting back, I let out a slow breath as the seconds passed.

But the message did not go through. There was only one logical explanation. Sarah was already in the air.

ME: *Rain check?*

As soon as I hit send, I changed my mind. Sarah lived in L.A. I lived in Houston. Even with me being a pilot, there was huge distance separating us.

Well. There was nothing I could do about it now. Unfortunately, there was no unsend button for unread text message. There should be.

At any rate, I had things to do.

I would have to figure out what to do about Sarah later.

43

SARAH

"This is a new antidepressant." I pushed half a dozen boxes of a fairly new drug across Dr. Meek's desk. "You might try them on a new patient, but I wouldn't try them with someone already on another antidepressant."

When he didn't answer, I kept going.

"It's intended for short term use. For people who need help dealing with a short-term situation. Sort of like antianxiety drugs. But for depression."

Dr. Meek was one of my favorite psychiatrists. Since we tended to think a lot alike, we'd hit it off from the start. I'd even met his wife and two young daughters. He had a lovely family.

His office always carried a calming scent of some kind of cinnamon spice and today I'd brought hot lattes for him and his staff. Together, it smelled like fall.

I'd been back in town for just over a week and it was almost like my trip to Houston had never happened.

I hadn't heard anything about my job application and other than a text suggesting a rain check, I had not heard from Luke.

I hadn't even responded to his text. A rain check? What

kind of response was that? I honestly did not even know what that meant.

Did it mean no or did it mean maybe later? Let me think about it.

Unless I got the job in Houston, it seemed like a moot point.

Luke wasn't going to fly all the way out here just to have brunch with me and I wasn't going to fly all the way to Houston to see him either.

That would just be crazy.

"Sarah," Dr. Meeks said, pulling my attention back to him.

"Yes?"

"Can I ask you a personal question?"

"Of course," I said with a little smile.

"Are you taking an antidepressant?" Dr. Meek leaned forward and smiled kindly at me.

"Yeah. No," I said, shaking my head and leaning back. Why was he asking me this?

He slowly slid one of the boxes of medicine in my direction.

"You might be a good candidate," he said.

"What? No. I'm not depressed."

Dr. Meek leaned back and shrugged.

"You don't seem like yourself. I thought maybe you were going through something that you might need help with."

I'd known Dr. Meek a long time. Several years now and he knew me fairly well.

Perhaps better than I had thought he knew me.

I had to admit that I'd been feeling a sadness weighing down my eyes. It didn't matter that I told myself that Luke had just been a passing fling.

I was very disciplined and avoided flings on my travels. I knew too many people who had gotten into various kinds of trouble, including getting their hearts broken. One colleague had even gotten pregnant. Now she was a single mother and had to take a lower paying job that didn't require travel.

Billionaire's Unexpected Landing 135

"I'll be okay," I said, forcing a smile. Dr. Meek was merely trying to be helpful.

He slid the box of medicine back next to the others.

"Seriously, though," he said. "If you ever need to talk, I'm here. Don't hesitate."

"You're very kind," I said. "And if I need to, I'll take you up on it."

As Dr. Meek's phone rang, I took the opportunity to excuse myself. I gathered up my bag and walking lightly on my heels to keep from being noticed, dashed out of his office, down the deserted hallway, and almost made it out the front door without being noticed.

"Leaving so soon?" Jeremy asked, stepping out of the little office he shared with the other intern. At the moment, instead of his white coat, he was wearing black slacks and a white shirt, unbuttoned at the collar.

"Yes," I said, catching my breath and forcing a small smile.

I went to step around him, but he stepped with me.

"Everything okay?" he asked.

"Of course."

"I was wondering if I could ask you about that medication you brought last time."

"Apologies, Jeremy," I said. "I'm just on my way back. Email me, okay?"

I moved past him again and this time he allowed me to pass.

"Sure," he said, as I clipped past him, not bothering anymore to walk lightly on my heels.

I tried to keep my customers happy. Anyone, even Jeremy, could become a future customer.

I'd make up for it when I came back next month. I'd bring coffee and something sweet. A cake maybe.

My meeting with Dr. Meek was eye-opening. I needed to get myself together.

As I rode down the elevator toward the garage I made a decision.

It was time for to take some time off.

My father had sold my grandfather's winery, but he still owned the house. I'd never taken him up on the offer to visit, but it was time.

It was probably vacant. It wouldn't take me long to find out. I'd ask Zachary for a few days off. Head up to the house in the country. Get myself together.

44

LUKE

*M*y Aunt Madison did not miss a thing.

Aunt Madison was a professor at a Denver university and she saw clients in her private practice on the side.

Growing up around both her and Grandma, I'd learned quite a bit about the way psychologists saw things. And, yes, it affected how I viewed the world. Just like aviation affected them.

But right now, my world did not look so good.

Madison sat right up front with me in the copilot's seat, wearing her headset and a pair of dark sunshades. If I hadn't known better, I would have thought she wasn't much older than me. She had most definitely held her age well.

She'd flown so much with her father and her husband Kade, that she could probably fly a plane all by herself if she had to.

"Something's bothering you," she said somewhere east of Colorado Springs, her voice coming in clear through my headset, interrupting my moment of brooding.

I shot her a smile that felt more like a grimace and probably looked like one. I added a shrug to the grimace.

"Not really."

"Okay." Madison looked away and didn't say anything else.

I knew what she was doing. She was giving me time to think about what I wanted to say. She knew that I'd tell her if she just waited it out.

"Are you on Fall break?" I asked, knowing the distraction was temporary. But I needed time to think. So I stalled.

"Something like that," she said.

It was rather unusual for her to travel to Houston in the middle of the week.

"Is everything okay?" I asked. Father hadn't told me *why* Aunt Madison was flying to Houston. She didn't have to have a reason. She and Kade hopped into a plane like the rest of the world hopped into their SUV. It was just that usually those trips revolved around her classes.

"Everything's fine," she said. "I just have a dentist appointment."

"Right." That actually made perfect sense. Madison and Kade still thought of Houston as their home for the most part. For the important things.

I'm sure I always would, too. I couldn't even contemplate ever living anywhere else. But if I did, Houston would remain my hometown. My base.

"I'll be okay," I said. Then took a deep breath and just blurted it out. "I met this girl."

Madison smiled knowingly. I hated when she did that.

"But?"

I sighed. "But she lives in L.A."

"So?"

"That's a long way."

"We fly to L.A. all the time."

She was right. The Worthingtons had relatives in L.A. including Grandpa's oldest daughter by his first wife. My Aunt Danielle.

Billionaire's Unexpected Landing 139

"It's still a long way," I said, going back into my brooding mood.

Madison lowered her shades and looked at me.

"You like this girl?"

"I guess she got under my skin," I said, shifting in my seat. Did I really want to tell anyone, even Aunt Madison that Sarah was all I'd been thinking about day? It was silly really.

There were millions of fishes in the sea, as they said. My missing her would fade over time.

"I'll be okay," I said again.

"I know you will," Aunt Madison said, taking out her iPad to read.

I guess the conversation was over.

That's when I realized I really did want to talk about Sarah.

45

SARAH

I left the next morning for what used to be Lawrence Valley Winery. It had long since changed names, but that didn't bother me. I just wanted to stay in the house. Maybe take some walks around the grounds.

My father used it on occasion as a getaway, but a quick conversation had given me clearance to use the house since Father was in France.

He'd never remarried, but I often thought he should have. Since my mother passed, he'd been a bit lost and not a little bit wild. He did whatever he wanted and whenever he wanted to do it. And that whatever usually involved being away from L.A.

The drive up to the winery—I'd always think of it that way even if my family no longer owned more than a couple of acres around the house—was peaceful.

Needing to be alone with my own thoughts, I didn't even turn on any music. As I drove, I went through a wide range of emotions.

Sadness at the loss of possibilities with Luke.

Then moved through a sense of freedom, mostly at being able to come up here and spend a few days. I could not

Billionaire's Unexpected Landing 141

remember the last time I had taken time off for myself. Any time off had involved work. I always had at least one or two work meetings with psychiatrists.

Then my thoughts wound their way back around to Luke.

I should be grateful to him for letting me know that I could still enjoy an evening with a handsome man. It had been too long.

Maybe after this weekend, I'd download one of those apps and figure out the whole swiping thing. But the thought depressed me, so I tucked it away.

I did not have to date. I was content with my life the way it was.

It hit me then. Right in the face. Perhaps I was more like my father than I'd ever wanted to admit.

No. I did not want that lifestyle. I did not want to be like my father, avoiding putting down roots. I understood why he was that way, but he must have some propensity toward it anyway or he would have settled down again.

Maybe meeting Luke was a kind of wakeup call. He was making me think about things I hadn't thought about in a while. Including my lifestyle.

Maybe I would get a pet. Not a dog because I traveled too much, but maybe a cat. Cats were self-sufficient, weren't they?

By the time I was driving down the lane leading to the house, I knew it wouldn't be fair to get a pet when I was gone half the time.

That depressed me, too. Maybe Dr. Meek was right. Maybe I did need to take some of my own medicine. Literally.

Seeing the house was bittersweet. Familiar. And with that familiarity came memories.

The house was a two-story manor built in the early twentieth century. A wide balcony with wooden railing jutted out across the front of house and a trail of green ivy wound its way up the post on the far right.

As I walked across the veranda toward the double doored entrance, I noticed that the white paint was starting to flake.

It was a shame that no one lived in the house. A house needed someone in it to keep it alive.

As much as it hurt my heart to think about, maybe I needed to talk to my father about selling the house.

He rarely came here and this place did not fit in with my lifestyle either. That realization hurt, too.

I dropped my keys on the little table in the foyer, looked around, and sighed.

I had so many things to think about.

46

LUKE

One of the things I loved the most about flying was that —with the exception of flying with Aunt Madison—I had a lot of time to myself to think.

That was also one of the few things I sometimes did not like about flying, at least at the moment anyway.

There wasn't much chatter on the radio today and on top of that today's flight had come with more turbulence than usual. It had been a short flight up to Dallas and back. It was a flight I made at least once a week, usually involving someone coming to or from the other Skye Travels up there.

Grandpa had started Skye Travels in Fort Worth, then as he and Grandma started their family—their large family of five children—they had moved to Houston and the company had grown even bigger.

As I flew out of the clouds, I had a good view of a thunderstorm coming off from the west. I would be on the ground long before it hit the Houston area.

I settled back and drank a sip of water.

So far I had been wrong.

It had been two days and I was still thinking about Sarah.

She had not responded to my rain check text—the one I wish I could take back.

I'd tried to think of something to say to erase it, but I didn't want to seem desperate. I thought about calling her, but I wasn't quite sure what I would say.

I'd replayed the whole morning over and over in my head and I had come to the conclusion that I had stood her up.

That was something I had never done before. Not to anyone.

I'd watched my sister get stood up for her date to the prom and I never wanted to put a girl through that kind of pain.

So I didn't call mostly because I was ashamed.

I couldn't even call to thank her for helping me out with Zoe. One, the thing with Zoe was still an unresolved mystery and two what kind of man called to thank a girl for kissing him?

I was in the worst kind of quandary I could imagine.

As the Houston airport came into view, I knew I needed to talk to somebody. Either my Grandma Savannah, or my Aunt Madison.

Going to a stranger to talk was out of the question. I trusted the two psychologists in my family.

It would be like Aunt Madison booking a flight with another airline or flying commercial.

We took care of our own.

So that's what I would do. Since I still needed to talk to Grandpa about the whole Zoe thing, I'd just head up to Grandpa and Grandma's house and kill two birds with one stone.

My wheels touched down in a perfect landing and, again, my thoughts landed on Sarah. The way she'd looked waiting for me outside that Abilene airport.

Now I couldn't even go in for a landing without thinking about her.

As I taxied down the runway toward the Skye Travels terminal and turned my cell phone back on, it populated with text messages.

A quick glance told me there was nothing from Sarah.

But unfortunately, I would not be going up to my grandparent's house tonight.

47

SARAH

*T*urns out I had a low tolerance for boredom.

It had not occurred to me that there would be no Internet out here at the winery.

The first twenty-four hours were the worst. I felt like I was in exile.

After that, I slowly began to adapt, but I did think about cutting my trip short or at least driving into the little neighboring town just to check my messages.

It wasn't that I was expecting anything important.

My father was in France, so he wouldn't be needing me.

Zachary knew where I was and although he was a demanding boss, he respected vacation time.

So that left Luke.

Even though the ball was in my court, I hoped he'd text again. Or call.

And as soon as the thought crossed through my head, I'd find something to distract myself.

I'd brought a book on psychotropic medications with me, but that only took the better part of a day to finish.

Billionaire's Unexpected Landing 147

With nothing left to do, I put my hands on my hips and surveyed the living room.

If we were going to even think about selling this house, someone had some work to do. And since I was here, I might as well see about getting started on it.

While I searched for boxes, I heard a vehicle pulling slowly around the circle drive. There was no through traffic here. Anyone who came here either had a very good reason or was lost. And even the people who were lost rarely made it this far before turning around.

Since I was upstairs, I went to the window and watched as a middle-aged man stepped out of the SUV and went around to the back. I didn't recognize him.

Then he pulled out a vase of red roses and started walking with no hesitation whatsoever toward the front door.

Red roses?

He was definitely lost. There was no one here to be getting flowers. But this delivery guy walked like he came here every day.

I needed to intercept him. To tell him he was making a mistake.

Heading into the hallway, I dashed down the stairs, but still, by the time I reached the front door, the man was already back in his SUV and pulling out of the driveway.

I didn't blame him. It was a long way out here and I was sure he was more than ready to get back to town.

I watched the vehicle until it turned and was out of sight, then I looked down at the flowers.

I couldn't leave them out here. It wasn't their fault they were at the wrong house.

Using both hands, I picked up the vase and took it inside, closing the door with my foot.

I put it on the table in the middle of the foyer and went back to lock the door.

Then I found the little white envelope tucked inside the flowers.

I stared blankly at the name printed on the outside.

Sarah Lawrence.

Only two people knew I was here. My father and Zachary. Neither one of them had any reason to send me flowers, especially not red roses.

It wasn't my birthday and it wasn't a holiday.

This was some kind of mistake.

My hands trembled as I opened the envelope and pulled out the card.

Until next time.

I dropped it onto the table next to the vase as though it had burned my fingers.

What the—?

I quickly found the phone number of the florist, but then I remembered that I had no cell service. That and there was no land line.

I had no way to call the florist to find out who had done this.

I wasn't dating anyone and hadn't for a while.

Unable to make sense of it, I double-checked the door lock. There had to an explanation. I'd drive into town tomorrow and go to the florist shop myself. Find out who had sent them.

Resolving to put it behind me, I continued my search for boxes.

I found some flat boxes in the laundry room, taped them together and made three boxes like everyone said to do.

One to donate.

One to toss.

And one to keep.

There was so much stuff... so many keepsakes... and sadly enough, not a one of them meant anything to me.

Billionaire's Unexpected Landing 149

My father's parents had passed long before I'd gotten a chance to know them.

It felt odd, going through their things, knowing that the things had meant something to them at one time, but now no one would ever know why.

I seriously doubted even my father would know why his parents had kept a jar full of sand.

I took it out back, emptied the sand on the ground, and put the jar in the donate box.

Then, on second thought, I moved it to the toss box. I couldn't think of anyone who would want an old jar like that.

A collector.

With a groan, I moved it back to the donate box.

Maybe this had been a bad idea.

I should have let my father do this.

But he would never do it. He'd just try to sell the house like it sat. He would get far more for it without the clutter.

Needing to take a break, went to the kitchen for a glass of water. Unfortunately, the roses permeated the air, grabbing my attention every time I walked near the foyer.

I grabbed a glass of water and went into the study. It smelled like vanilla and a deep woodsy scent. There was an oversized desk angled so the user had a good view of what used to be the flower garden.

At some point the study had also served as a library. There was a row of bookshelves along one wall, crammed with books. Old leather-bound books. Paperback books. Some never opened. Some tattered from being read over and over.

I picked a tattered paperback and flipped through it. It was an old romance western. I wondered whether it had been my grandmother or my grandfather that had read it.

I set it back on the shelf and took a deep breath.

That was going to be a nightmare to clear out.

I'd have to donate them to a library. That would be hard,

but there was no way I could keep them all. One or two maybe at the most.

I sat down at the roll top desk and slowly slid it open.

It was surprisingly organized. And my first impression was that it belonged to a female.

There was a little pink and green mug filled with pens with ink that had dried up long ago. There was a little clock that no longer worked.

And there was a little flowery box tied with a white ribbon.

I sat my water bottle aside and carefully removed the ribbon.

The little box was filled with letters.

Fighting that sense of intrusion at looking through someone else's private things, I picked up one of the envelopes and carefully removed the letter, the paper crisp with age.

48

LUKE

*I*t had been one of those long nights that I would not wish on my worst enemy.

My grandmother, Savannah Worthington, lay in the hospital bed, her skin pale, her eyes closed. She'd been dozing on and off since I got here yesterday.

Everyone else had gone home, but I had stayed. Someone would be here to take my place in a couple of hours. Probably my Aunt Ainsley or Aunt Madison. With so many family members, Grandma would never have a moment alone.

The monitors beeped steadily, assuring me that she was okay, at least for the moment.

Grandma had been working with a client when it had started. She'd apparently starting talking about something completely irrelevant, though none of us knew what it was.

Then she had turned around thrown up in her wastebasket.

The poor client who had come to talk about her own problems, had recognized that something was terribly wrong and called 911.

Grandma had been in the midst of a heart attack. I'd never known her to be sick a day in her life.

When I got there, Grandpa had been beside himself with worry. Pacing around the room. Barking at the nurses to get the doctor back in there.

Like me, Grandpa had been flying when it had all happened. He'd gotten to the hospital less than an hour before I did.

In fact, right now, he was asleep, his feet hanging over the end of the little sofa on the other side of the hospital room.

One of the nurses had draped a blanket over him and I think they had given him something to help him sleep.

Otherwise, I was certain he would still be sitting at Grandma's side, holding her hand.

Tomorrow... later today actually... they would be doing tests to determine whether or not she would need heart surgery.

It hurt me more than I could put in words to see my grandmother lying there hooked up to monitors. She didn't look old enough to be a grandmother. Like my aunts, she was aging slowly. Good genes, I suppose. And not a little bit of happiness in life.

I stared out at the nurses' station, watching them going about their business. This was just a job to them. Like flying a plane was to me.

I was developing a new appreciation for passengers who were nervous about flying. To me it was fun and exciting, but they were terrified. Just like I was right now.

"Luke?"

My gaze jerked back to Grandma.

"Grandma." I took her hand and my eyes welled with moisture.

"Where's Noah?" she asked, her voice hoarse.

"Sleeping." I nodded toward the sofa.

She turned her head and looked toward her husband with a little smile.

"Good," she said. "I worry about him."

Billionaire's Unexpected Landing   153

I didn't bother to tell her that she was the one everyone was worried about. She had to know it, but it was just like her to be worried about everyone else instead of herself.

"How long have I been in here?" she asked. "I've lost track of time."

"Since yesterday," I said, running a hand over my face.

She nodded. "It seems like forever."

I smiled a little at that. "It seems like forever to me, too."

She squeezed my hand.

"You look troubled," she said.

"I have good reason to," I said, nodding once toward her.

She shook her head.

"No. It's not that." Her brow furrowed, emphasizing the little creases at the corners of her eyes.

Grandma was an amazing woman. Even now, lying in a hospital bed, her own life in peril, she was working.

She couldn't help it. It was in her blood.

"Tell me about her," she said.

49

SARAH

Two hours later, I sat cross legged in the floor of the study, handwritten papers all around me.

I'd sorted them. Some had been written by my great-great-grandfather and some had been written by my great-great-grandmother. That part had been easy since her writing was neat and small and his was larger and harder to read. Also, her letters were torn and tattered.

Then I'd sorted them by date.

Now that I had two stacks of letters, went about the business of weaving together to make a story.

Since I had been five years old when my mother passed, I did not have a good sense of my parents together. I only knew my father's anguish followed by his wildness.

I knew my grandparents some, but as the women in my family had a tendency to die early, I mostly knew my two grandfathers.

Now that I thought about it, it didn't give me much optimism about my own longevity.

Feeling all out of sorts, I went into the kitchen and made

myself a taco. As a frequent traveler, I rarely made my own food except on weekends and then I kept it simple.

As I sat at the breakfast table, eating lunch, I wondered if maybe I should have gone someplace with fewer memories. Maybe I should have gone to Disney World. But that was no fun alone.

My thoughts circled back around to the flowers and who could possibly have sent them. I was coming up empty-handed. Even thinking back through all the boyfriends I'd ever had, I hadn't brought any of them up here.

Tired of my own thoughts, I picked up the television remote and turned on the news. It didn't do much to cheer me up, but it distracted me sufficiently.

After lunch, I cleaned everything up and taking my stack of handwritten letters, went into the parlor, turned a lamp and settled in to read.

The first one was from my great-great-grandfather.

It was dated 1918.

My Dearest Rebecca,

Although I've only been away from you for a few days, I miss you terribly.

He gave a brushstroke picture of basic training. He had a couple of good friends, so it didn't sound so bad.

With fondest regards,

Nathaniel

It seemed like such a formal letter and if he'd begun with anything stating how much he missed her, I would have thought she was a family member. I reminded myself that it was written over one hundred years ago. A time when people dressed and spoke more formally than these days of text messages.

I set his letter aside and picked up the letter from Rebecca. It had obviously been handled more, probably carried around in a pocket.

Dear Nathaniel,

Interesting that Rebecca's salutation was more reserved.

Although we only had two days together, I feel like I've known you a much longer time.

I dropped the letter in my lap and stared outside toward where the vineyards had been.

I imagined my great-great grandmother sitting here, penning this letter to a man she obviously barely knew.

Only two days?

How was it they had ended up married?

I kept reading, getting lost in their correspondence, piecing together their story.

It seems like I've known you forever.

The memory of your kisses comforts me during the perils of battle.

I'm coming home, but I only have two days before I return. Will you marry me?

I caught my breath.

This was before the days of telephones and Internet.

Nathaniel was proposing to her by letter.

And after they had only known each other for two days.

I put the letter down and walked to the window.

There was a storm brewing. The wind sent a layer of dust through the air, giving everything a hazy appearance. Like an old photograph.

Heavy dark clouds hung on the horizon, making their way here.

Nathaniel and Rebecca's story sounded so heart wrenchingly familiar.

Two days.

That's how long Luke and I had known each other.

And in another time and place those letters could have been written by us.

50

LUKE

My wheels touched down on the little runway at the Abilene Airport. A smooth landing as always, despite the west Texas wind that plagued this part of the state. I loved Texas as much as any Texan, but personally I could do without the western part.

Strange as hell that I'd be dropping someone off in Abilene just days after I had picked Sarah up here at this same airport.

It was kind of surreal being here. I couldn't help looking for her, even though I knew she wasn't from here and had no reason to ever be here again.

"Thanks a bunch, Luke," Drake Grant said, before he headed down the stairs to the tarmac. Drake only flew with us a couple of times a year. He worked for himself, in some kind of advertising and unlike most of our passengers, he always wore jeans and a leather jacket. Kept to himself. Traveled light.

"Always a pleasure," I said. "Take care of yourself."

I waited until Drake was on his way across the tarmac before closing the door to the airplane and going back to sit in the pilot's seat.

My grandmother Savannah had gotten a lucky break. The

doctors said it was a mild heart attack causing hardly any damage to her heart. They gave her some medication and sent her on her way. With orders to rest for six weeks.

The words *Savannah Worthington* and *rest* clashed when put in the same sentence, but from all reports so far she was following doctor's orders.

If I had to guess, I'd say she was probably long overdue a rest. I'd heard a rumor that she and Grandpa were planning a trip up to their Colorado home whenever she felt up to it.

I went down my checklist. Everything was ready for takeoff. My flight plan was registered for Houston.

I unlocked my cell and pulled up Sarah's name.

After talking to Grandma, Grandpa had made a call to Mr. Madris who then made a call to a fellow named Zachary out in L.A.

It had taken no time at all for me to have Sarah's home address.

I also knew that she had taken some time off.

It had taken a little more digging, but I was pretty sure she was at her family's country home outside of L.A.

I had that address, too.

I was fairly certain that the only reason I had this information was because of Grandpa. I hoped it was the only reason. I hated to think that it would be this easy to locate someone, particularly Sarah, otherwise.

A jet took off in front of me, reminding me that I should get moving.

Grandma's words played clearly in my head.

Sometimes love came like a bolt of lightning. When you know, you know.

I pushed my dark sunshades up to the top of my head and stared at the address in my phone.

This was one of those times when I didn't know whether or not to follow my gut. It was funny because I rarely doubted

Billionaire's Unexpected Landing 159

myself when it came to women. But I'd never been hit by a bolt of lightning before.

With a sound that I wasn't sure was a laugh or a growl or maybe something else, I grabbed my iPad, cancelled my flight back to Houston, then entered a new flight path.

I got an immediate call from the Skye Travels office making sure I meant to do that.

While I was on the phone with them, I asked the receptionist to cancel my flights for the rest of the week. I rarely ever took advantage of being the boss's son. In fact, I couldn't remember ever doing it.

But a man had to do what a man had to do.

Who was I to question being hit by a bolt of lightning?

51

SARAH

I was probably the only person who had ever taken a flower arrangement *into* a flower shop.

It had been an ordeal to buckle the glass vase full of roses into the passenger seat so they wouldn't tump over.

When I got to the door of the little flower shop on Main Street of the little town, I had to set them down to open the door.

A middle-aged kindly looking woman hurried over to help me.

She held the door while I brought the flowers into the store. It wasn't a very big shop, so a quick glance told me I was the only customer.

There were lots of empty vases and candles sitting around on tables, but most of the flowers were in refrigerated cases.

Once inside, she took the heavy vase from me and set it on the nearest table.

"What's wrong with the flowers?" she asked, putting on the glasses hanging around her neck to peer at the rose buds.

"Nothing," I said, feeling like I was doing something wrong.

Billionaire's Unexpected Landing 161

Letting her glasses fall back down, she looked at me questioningly.

"They aren't mine," I said.

The woman put her glasses back on and searched for the card.

I pulled it out of my back jeans pocket and handed it to her.

"Do you know Sarah Lawrence?" she asked.

"I'm Sarah," I said.

"Well, then," she said. "They belong to you."

I took a deep breath and crossed my arms.

"Can you at least tell me who sent them?" I asked. "There's no name on the card."

"It's quite romantic," she said with a smile.

"No," I insisted. "It's not romantic. I don't know anyone who would send me flowers."

"You have a secret admirer." The woman put a hand on her chest.

"No. I don't." I shook my head. "Please just look it up and tell me who sent them."

"I'm so sorry," she said. "I can't do that."

"Look," I said, putting a hand on my forehead. "Someone obviously knows my name and where to find me. I'm out there all alone."

The woman just looked at me.

"I'm sure they were sent with the best of intents," she said, finally.

"Then they should have signed the card," I said.

When she didn't move, I tried one more time.

"Will you look? I just need to know who sent them."

"I don't have access to that information. The order came through an online company."

"Well," I said. "I don't want them so you can have them back."

The woman gaped at me.

"You should take them and enjoy them," she said.

"I'll just keep the card," I said, holding out my hand.

She put the card in my hand.

I turned on my heel and left the flower shop. By the time I reached my car, I realized I was trembling.

I sat in the driver's seat, squeezing the steering wheel with both hands.

It was unsettling. It was even more unsettling that she would not tell me who sent the flowers. I felt like I was out here on my own. All alone in this. Whatever this was.

I picked up my phone.

There had been no messages to speak of on my phone. A couple of text messages from my phone company. And the normal notices from my credit card charges.

Nothing important.

No calls or emails about the job in Houston.

On so many levels, it was looking more and more like that trip had never happened.

The job.

Luke.

Ready to get home now, I made a quick stop by the little market and drove back to the house.

The anonymous flowers had me thinking about going back home to L.A., but that just made me mad.

I still had things I wanted to do here. I was making progress on going through things getting it ready to stage.

Even if Father didn't want to put it up for sale right now, my grandparents' things still needed to be dealt with. As they should have been a long time ago. Since my father was an only child and I was an only child, it fell on my shoulders to do. Something I had not even realized until now.

Because I was taking my time, I'd found things like the letters written over a hundred years ago between my great-great-grandparents. It gave me chills just thinking about that.

Those letters gave a connection to my family that I had never had before.

I drove through the winery that we no longer owned. The plants looked healthy enough and I wondered how the company was doing.

I didn't know the new owners well enough to ask them and it wasn't my business anyway. Once something was sold, it was no longer yours to be concerned about. I know privacy was important to me, so I respected the privacy of others.

Back at the house, I parked around back and went in through the back door.

I filled a glass with water and drank it while I stood at the kitchen window.

I was still feeling out of sorts. I may never know who sent me those flowers and I hated that. I hated that if I didn't find out, that puzzle would be hanging over my head for the rest of my life.

And that made me determined to not think about it.

I grabbed my keys, locked up, and took a walk. It had a been a while since I'd gone to the gym. That was definitely one of the downsides to traveling so much. It made it difficult to keep up any kind of routine, especially fitness.

I walked along a path behind the house that made a circle around the edge of the property.

The sun was warm on my skin. Almost too warm, especially since I was wearing jeans. About halfway through my walk, I rolled up the sleeves of my chambray button-down shirt.

When the house came back into view, I slowed.

There was a car I didn't recognize sitting out in the front of the drive. It was a regular four-door white sedan.

I stopped. My feet freezing on their own accord, my fingers wrapping around the keys in my pocket. The door was locked so no one could get inside the house.

The light wind cooled my skin and tousled my hair. I

shoved it impatiently out of my eyes. My heart was pounding dangerously.

Although no one could get inside the house, I was out here, alone, with no way of defending myself.

I considered my options. I could hide behind a tree and wait, but that just seemed cowardly. I could make it to my car, but I hadn't brought my car key.

I squared my shoulders.

Whoever it was, I would just find out what they wanted.

It was the flowers. The flowers had me nervous and out of sorts.

Then I saw a man walking back towards the car.

He stopped and turned towards me.

My breath hitched and my brain struggled to catch up.

I knew him.

Luke.

52

LUKE

Once I had made my decision, I ran head with it.

It was the way I was built. There was really no other choice.

My father had waited years for Mother. During that time he had never faltered. Even though he hadn't known where she was, he hadn't even dated anyone else. I'd never really understood that.

Until now.

And then there was my grandfather, Noah Worthington—the man who had created the empire that was Skye Travels. His first business venture. One he jumped into with both feet, never hesitating.

My DNA was wired for not hesitating once I made up my mind.

So I blamed my father and my grandfather for standing at the country home of Sarah Lawrence.

If she didn't want to see me, I'd drive back to L.A. and fly myself back to Houston.

But seeing here again. Standing there with the light wind

tousling her hair around her face. I knew I would give it everything I had before I gave up.

I'm not sure which one of us moved first. I think we both started walking toward each other at the same time, our gazes locked onto each other.

Seconds later, I was standing in front of her.

"Hi," I said.

"Hi... What are you doing here?" she asked.

Such a complicated question I didn't know how to answer it.

"I think I owe you an apology."

She nodded. "For what?"

I smiled. "I think I promised you brunch."

"It was just a suggestion," she said with a shrug, before looking away. "Besides, I had to come back to L.A. for a meeting."

I couldn't read her. Couldn't figure out if she was upset with me or happy to see me...

"Can I make it up to you?" I asked.

When she smiled, her whole face lit up. With the sunshine on her hair, she was even more beautiful than I remembered... if that was possible.

"Maybe," she said.

It was all the encouragement I needed. I pulled her into a hug, wrapping my arms around her.

She wrapped her arms around my waist and rested her cheek against chest. She was wearing sneakers, so her head fit perfectly beneath my chin.

The seconds ticked past, then she pulled back and looked up at me.

"How did you find me?"

There was something in her eyes. Confusion. And what looked like worry.

"My grandfather made some calls."
She nodded, then laid her cheek back on my chest.
"It's good to see you," I said.

53

SARAH

*I*t was surreal having Luke here.

After I got over being terrified, I'd thought I was imagining things. Hallucinating maybe.

Only two people knew where to find me.

Or so I thought.

Apparently there were more than I knew.

The person who sent me flowers was the third.

And Luke appeared to be the fourth.

Unless...

I pulled back and searched his eyes. All I saw there was kindness and affection.

"When did you find out I was here?"

"Yesterday," he said. "Just before five o'clock."

He seemed to sense that I needed specifics.

I mentally did the calculations. That meant he couldn't be the one who sent the flowers.

My heart was still racing, but I smiled.

He moved his hands to cup my face. Then his lips were on mine. Soft. Gentle.

Just like I remembered.

Billionaire's Unexpected Landing   169

I sank into the kiss. Needing him. Needing everything about him.

I hadn't thought I would see him again.

Even if I got the job in Houston—which I had not heard anything yet—I still would not have felt comfortable contacting him.

Even if my heart wanted me to believe otherwise, in my head I had decided that he was one of those fly by night kinds of guys. Playing games.

I didn't blame him, really. Nobody in their right mind went into a long-distance relationship on purpose.

It was something a person just sort of fell into.

Yet here he was.

Standing right here with me.

And for just a minute I forgot about the card in my back pocket.

The one that someone who wasn't supposed to know or care where I was had sent with a beautiful bouquet of red roses.

"This place is beautiful," he said, pulling me against him again. "Is it yours?"

"No," I said, feeling the loss deep in my gut. I'd never really felt much ownership of my family's land. Probably because my father had sold most of it. So that visceral sense of loss came at me as a complete surprise.

"My father kept the house," I clarified. "But this is the winery he sold when my mother got sick."

"Right," he said, instinctively stroking the back of my head in a comforting gesture.

It actually helped. I began to feel more settled and relaxed in his arms.

As we stood there, the sun began to set, splashing reds and golds across the sky.

"It's so beautiful," I said.

"What's that?" He murmured absently.

"The sky." I leaned back and looked into his eyes again. "Do you want to go inside?" I asked.

54

LUKE

The Lawrence country home wasn't what I expected, although I couldn't have said exactly what it was that I did expect.

The house didn't appear to have a lot of life in it. Coming in through the back door, we'd passed a couple of rooms with covered furniture. I hated seeing a house closed down like this. A house was supposed to be full of family and life.

But the parlor she led me to resembled a normal enough house other than the three half-filled boxes on one side of the room.

"Doing some packing?" I asked, with a slight nod toward the boxes.

"Just sorting through some old things that belonged to my grandparents," she said, picking up a stack of old magazine from the sofa and moving them to the floor. "My father never did it."

"He probably didn't want to deal with it," I said.

The idea of having to go through my parents' things was unthinkable. With four siblings and a host of aunts and uncles, at least, I knew it was never something I would have to do alone.

"Do you have anyone to help you?" I asked. "Brothers or sisters?"

"I'm an only child," she said. "But don't hold it against me." She sat on the sofa and gave me a half smile.

"I won't," I said, sitting next to her. "But I gotta tell you. I can't even imagine what it might be like."

"Right," she said. "You have a big family."

"You should see our family gatherings," I said.

"And that's something I can't imagine." She smiled wistfully.

"It's almost like we come from different worlds," I said, covering her hand with mine and giving it a squeeze. "But I don't mind if you don't."

"I don't mind," she said, picking up a glass of water from the end table. She looked at it, then set it back down after seeming to have second thoughts about drinking it.

I pulled my phone out of my pocket and scowled at the lack of service.

"No service out here?" I asked.

"Unfortunately, no. I was surprised, too."

"I had service on the drive up." I was accustomed to not having service in the air, but rarely on the ground.

"I think it ends about a mile or so toward town."

I tapped my phone and wondered how often I was going to drive that mile just to check my messages.

"Something important?" she asked.

"Yes, actually," I said. "It's been a rather eventful few days."

"What's happened?" she asked, leaning forward.

"My grandmother…" I stopped. Saying it out loud made it all the more real. Too real.

"Is she okay?"

I took a deep breath. "Yes. She is now. She had a heart attack and is home now. But I still worry about her."

"Oh my God," she said. "A heart attack. Why are you here?" She put a hand on my arm. "Instead of there?"

"She has enough people around her. Too many, really." I took her hand in mine and kissed the soft part of her palm. "Besides. I wanted to see you."

I didn't want to think about my grandmother or work or anything right now other than Sarah.

55

SARAH

*L*uke's lips were sending tingles along my spine.

"I didn't really plan on having guests." I said, mostly to distract myself from wanting to kiss him again.

He looked up at me with a rather stunned expression and released my hand.

Damn it. I had not meant to make him feel unwelcome. He was actually more than welcome. I didn't want to seem overly ecstatic, but to say that I was pleased was an understatement.

"I don't really have any food," I said, quickly to make amends for the comment he seemed to be taking the wrong way.

"We can go into the little town," he said, with a little smile. "I saw a market and a little café on the way in."

"Right," I said. "We can do that. And we can check our phone messages."

He grinned. "You're a woman after my own heart."

I smiled again. It seemed like I was always smiling from just being near him.

But then I bit my bottom lip.

Billionaire's Unexpected Landing 175

"You flew all the way out to L.A. and drove up here just to see me?" And what I didn't say was that he didn't even know whether or not I would want to see him.

"Yes," he said. "That's one thing you have to know about pilots. We'll take any excuse we can find to fly somewhere." He sat back and stretched out his long legs.

"I see," I said.

This conversation seemed to be putting us at odds. He wasn't sure I wanted him here and I wasn't sure he hadn't just used me as an excuse to take a flight to California to see some wine country.

"Wait here," I said. "I want to show you something."

I went to the study and brought the letters from my great-great-grandparents back into the parlor.

"What's that?" he asked, sitting up straighter.

"Letters written over one hundred years ago," I said. settling on the sofa with my feet under me. "By my great-great-grandparents. I sorted them by date."

"You've been busy," he said, looking over at the letters. "So some are written by her and some are written by him?"

"It makes a little narrative of their relationship." I said, picking up the first letter. "He wrote first."

"Can I read it?" he asked, holding out a hand.

"Of course." I handed him the letter and he began to read.

"*My Dearest Rebecca,*" he read out loud. "*Although I've only been away from you for a few days, I miss you terribly.*"

He paused and looked up at me with a curious expression.

A little shiver shot up my spine. I watched him closely as he continued reading.

"*With fondest regards, Nathaniel.*"

At end of the letter, he looked at me.

I swallowed thickly and chewed my bottom lip. Something about hearing him say the words written by my ancestor tugged at my heart. Words that professed how much he missed me even though we had only been apart a few days. Though the words belonged to someone else, they could so easily be his.

My hands trembling a little, I picked up the next letter. This one written by Rebecca.

Luke watched me closely, his gaze warming my skin.

"Dear Nathaniel." I glanced up at him and cleared my throat.

He was smiling at me with a sideways grin. I lowered my gaze and continued to read.

"Although we only had two days together, I feel like I've known you a much longer time."

I took a deep breath and felt my cheeks heat. Again, the words, even though they weren't mine, rang true as to how I felt about Luke.

I kept reading.

"It saddens my heart to know that you are there. On your way to fight in a battle."

I lost myself in my great-great-grandmother's words, hypnotized almost by her prose.

"Yours truly." I looked up into Luke's eyes. *"Rebecca."*

As he picked up the next letter written by Nathaniel, he leaned over and kissed me lightly on the lips.

"My lovely Rebecca," he read. *"I miss you terribly."*

I watched as he continued to read.

We went through each letter, one by one.

"It seems like I've known you forever," I read.

The minutes turned in hours.

"The memory of your kisses comforts me during the perils of battle."

He paused and looked up at me, gazing at me with his intent blue eyes. I could fall into those eyes and never come out.

Finishing the letter, he set the letter aside. "Your turn," he said.

Billionaire's Unexpected Landing   177

"I need something to drink," I said, uncurling myself and standing up from the sofa.

"Oh," he said. "I have something in the car." He stood up. "I'll be right back."

As he headed to his car, I took my glass to the kitchen and filled it with fresh water. I had forgotten to buy bottles of water, but the tap water tasted fine to me.

Luke came right on back in from outside.

"I didn't come empty handed," he said, holding up a bottle of cabernet. "This was the best I could find at the little market in town."

"Oh wow," I said, taking the bottle from him. "I didn't think about them having wine there."

He looked at me sideways. "In wine country?"

I just shrugged. "I hardly even think about it like that."

"Shall I open it?" he asked.

"Please." I looked around. "There's got to be corkscrew around here somewhere."

Luke walked over to one of the cabinets beneath a little wine rack and opened the drawer.

"Found some," he said, holding up three different corkscrews.

I laughed as I pulled two wine glasses from the cabinet.

Luke opened the wine and filled the two glasses.

"It's not bad," I said taking a sip.

He put his arm around me.

"I guess I got lucky," he said, kissing me on the top of the head.

56

LUKE

*S*ara sat on the sofa, her feet stretched out and I sat on the floor behind her as we continued to read the letters written by her great-great-grandparents.

I never would have thought I'd find reading old letters entertaining, but the way we were reading them as though we had been the ones to write them was tantalizing and more than entertaining.

It was even more interesting reading the letters while drinking the smooth cabernet.

It was my turn to read. I noticed that as the letter continued, Nathaniel got more and more bold with his words and that the two of them fed upon each other, each saying more and more about how they felt.

"If you have a photograph, would you send it to me?"

I looked over my shoulder at Sarah. "Too bad she can't just send him a selfie, huh?"

"A hundred years makes all the difference."

"You're the first thing I think about when I wake up in the morning and the last thing I thing I think about before I fall asleep at night."

I stopped, giving myself a moment for the lump in my throat to go away. I did the same thing. Thinking about Sarah when I woke in the morning and at night before I went to sleep.

I looked over my shoulder again. "They couldn't even call each other on the phone, could they?" I was trying to make light of it, but in truth, I was feeling emotional.

"I think this was before telephones." Her own voice came out soft and breathy.

"I know," I said. "But it seems like the more they write to each other the closer they're becoming.

"It's almost like they're having a correspondence romance," she said. "Except they've already met."

"So they already know they like each other."

"It's almost like they backed off when he first went away, and now they're coming back to where they were. Before he left."

"I long for the day when I see you again." I paused as Nathaniel moved to the next paragraph. *"I have to go now. It's time for reveille."*

I dropped the paper into my lap. "He's writing her first thing in the morning."

"What's wrong with that?" she asked.

"Nothing," I said. But a man who would get up early in the morning to make sure he had time to write his girl was truly smitten.

"It must mean something to you," she said, straightening behind me. "You seem surprised."

"No," I said. "It just makes him seem so much more real."

"He was real," she said softly.

"It's just these people back in World War I were probably one of America's greatest generations."

"I agree," she said. "It sort of feels like intruding on their private worlds."

"Maybe," I said. "It feels like an honor to me. To get to hear their thoughts. How their relationship progressed."

I hadn't planned on reading all the letters, but now that we were into them, I didn't want to stop. I wanted to see what they said to each other next.

57

SARAH

We took a break from reading.

Went back to the kitchen to make something to eat.

"It's unfortunate there's no pizza delivery out here," I said as I turned on the gas cooktop to make grilled cheese sandwiches.

"I think you and I were made for each other," he said. "But a grilled cheese sandwich is good, too."

I laughed. But if he was going to keep making comments like this, he was going to have me thinking we were more than just two people who just met.

Just like Nathaniel and Rebecca.

I shrugged off the thought and put the bread in the skillet, butter side down.

I'd brought the makings for grilled cheese sandwiches, coffee, and popcorn. I figured I could live off that for a few days. Plus there was a market not too far away.

"More wine?" he asked.

"Maybe later," I said with a little smile over my shoulder. I didn't need my brain fogged up by alcohol when already it was hard to think around Luke.

"Want to try the little café tomorrow for dinner?" he asked.

"Sure," I said, trying to sound casual. He hadn't said how long he was planning on staying. Obviously a couple of nights. But where? Was he planning to stay here?

He got out two plates while I grilled the sandwiches.

A comfortable silence settled over us as we sat at the little kitchen table to eat.

Darkness had moved in, bringing a coolness to the air, even inside the house.

"Did you ever figure out what was going on with Zoe?" I asked.

He shook his head. "It didn't come up again. With my grandmother in the hospital and all."

"Right." That would have taken precedence over everything else. But I think, if it had been me, I would have figured out why my father wanted me to marry a girl I barely knew before I flew out here to spend time with someone else.

"I'll sort it out," he said, with a little shrug.

Sometimes men were funny creatures the way they didn't worry about things, especially things that could be life changing.

"I saw a little inn when I drove through town," he said. "After we clean up here, I'll drive back down there and get a room for the night."

"Okay," I said, mostly because I was annoyed with him for not being worried about his family's wishes for him to marry Zoe.

He finished his sandwich, then finished his wine.

"No flight tomorrow?"

"No." He grinned.

Jet lag, I decided, and wine did not mix.

"I think you better stay here," I said, then quickly added. "In the guest room."

"I don't want to impose," he said.

Billionaire's Unexpected Landing　　　　183

"It's a big house," I said. "There's plenty of room."

I didn't know if staying here with me had been his intent all along or if going back to the inn had been his intent.

Judging by how little he concerned himself about an arranged marriage, I couldn't imagine that where he slept for the night was very high on his priority list of things to plan.

"It's a deal then," he said. "But only if you let me take you to dinner tomorrow night."

I nodded. I didn't blame him. I doubted there were very many nights when Luke Worthington ate nothing more than a grilled cheese sandwich. Not a bad thing. I could probably say the same about myself.

"I'll go get the guest room ready," I said, getting up and tossing my half-eaten sandwich in the trash can.

"I'll help you," he said.

"Yeah. No. No. Just stay here and relax for a few minutes. I'll be right back."

I needed to get away from him for a minute. To think.

Luke had me twisted up on the inside.

My paltry dinner was a scalding reminder that he might not be a billionaire, but his family was. And that meant he would be some day, even if he wasn't now.

58

LUKE

I let Sarah go. I had no choice, anyway.

Something was suddenly bothering her.

While I waited for her to come back, I washed the dishes.

She was right when she implied that I didn't need to drive. I'd only had a glass and a half of wine, but I didn't like driving the least bit impaired.

I hadn't thought through where I was going to stay. I hadn't gotten that far.

I'd only known that I wanted to see Sarah. To spend time with her. I knew I'd figure it out from there.

Planning wasn't my strong point. I got that from my grandfather. Apparently I'd gotten the his laisse faire gene in place of my father's anal retentive planning gene. That one had just skipped right over me.

It was a little bit odd, since as a pilot I had to keep something of a schedule. But outside of my flights and my family, of course, I didn't impose a whole lot of structure on myself. I'd never seen the need.

Compared to my brother, Dylan, though, I most definitely seemed structured.

Billionaire's Unexpected Landing 185

"Okay," Sarah said, coming back into the kitchen. "The sheets aren't exactly fresh, but they're clean."

She stopped and looked from me to the empty sink.

"You did the dishes?" she asked, surprise evident in her voice. "And put them up?"

"Yeah," I said with a shrug.

"You didn't have to." She seemed a bit disconcerted by the fact that I had washed the dishes.

"It was no problem."

"Thank you," she said.

I went over and took her hands, waiting until her gaze met mine.

"Hey," I said, sweeping her hair back from her face and tucking it over her left shoulder. "Are you okay?"

She nodded, but I could see the shadows in her green eyes. Something was bothering her.

"I didn't come here with a plan to impose on you," I said. "I just wanted to see you."

"You're not imposing," she said, with a little smile.

I pulled her into a hug. "You can tell me anything," I said. "Okay?"

"Okay," she murmured against my chest.

I don't know why I had a feeling something was bothering her. I hadn't known her long enough to know the nuances of her moods .

It was just one of those things. A feeling.

Maybe we were both just tired from reading the letters between Nathaniel and Rebecca.

"I'll bring in my luggage, then we probably need to get some sleep."

"Sounds like a good idea," she said, looking up at me.

I ran a finger across her cheek and cupped the back of her head before placing a kiss on her lips.

It was several hours later, though, before we headed up the

stairs to our respective rooms.

59

SARAH

*A*fter changing into my pajamas, I climbed into bed and settled in beneath the warm comforter. Leaning back against a big oversized pillow and, picking up the novel I was reading, opened it up to where I had left off last night.

Sometimes I read online, on my iPad or my iPhone, but other times I liked the feel of a paper book in my hands, preferably a hardback book.

But I didn't read. The words blurred on the page.

This had been a most eventful day, taking my emotions all over the place.

First there had been the trip into town to the flower shop. It had been most disappointing to not have an answer to who sent me the flowers. It was almost like there was a HIPPA for flower shops.

I had not told Luke about it and I certainly had not asked him if he was the one who sent them. That didn't fit. I was almost positive he hadn't sent them, but damn it, there would always be that little lingering doubt that came from not knowing.

Then there was Luke. I never in a million years would have thought he would show up here.

When he hadn't shown up at the airport, I had given up on seeing him again. His raincheck text was a blow off I'd used myself a number of times. To me it meant *thanks, but no thanks.*

Then he had shown up here and I had been completely caught off guard.

It was a little disconcerting that he had been able to find me. If it had been anyone else, I would have been more than disconcerted. I would have been concerned. But Luke's family ran in the same circles as Mr. Madris, the guy I'd interviewed with.

So from there, I had not been hard to find. I was going to have a word with Zachary, though, about giving out my personal information without asking me first.

I sighed. He might have called. If he had, I would not have known. No cell phone service out here. Maybe he had been concerned about me after he couldn't reach me. I could come up with all sorts of reasons why he would have given Noah Worthington my address out here.

But the bottom line was, I didn't mind.

I was actually flattered that Luke had gone to the trouble not only to find out where I was, but to fly all the way out to L.A., then make the drive out here to the winery.

I couldn't keep from smiling a little as I replayed the last couple of hours spent kissing him.

I could kiss him for days without stopping. Our lips molded together so perfectly.

Deciding I'd rather think about kissing Luke than read, I closed the book, all but forgotten in my lap.

I turned off the lamp and snuggled beneath the blankets.

We hadn't talked about his being here. I almost felt like talking to him about it would somehow break the spell. I had a feeling that even if I did ask, he wouldn't an answer.

Billionaire's Unexpected Landing

My gut told me that he wouldn't answer because he couldn't.

If I was right, he didn't know. We were just playing it by ear, seeing how things went.

I really didn't mind that so much. I wanted to see how things went, too.

And right now, knowing that Luke was in the room next door, I felt completely safe.

60

LUKE

*W*earing my running pants, t-shirt, and running sneakers, I got up with the sun and headed downstairs.

If there was phone service only a mile away, I could kill two birds with one stone. Get some exercise and check my messages.

As I crossed through the foyer, I noticed Sarah's phone, on charge, on a little side table. If I knew her better... much better... I'd take her phone with me and let her messages come in, too.

A card next to her phone caught my attention. It wasn't the card itself. It looked like an ordinary card that came with flowers. But then it occurred to me that she might have another man interested in her. She'd said she had no boyfriend, but that didn't mean she didn't have friends who wanted to be boyfriends.

She probably had a lot of guys interested in her, though I didn't get a sense that she was anything like Zoe with a dozen guys hanging around her, competing for her attention.

Billionaire's Unexpected Landing 191

In fact, as hard as I tried, I couldn't imagine Zoe coming up here to spend time alone. I doubted she rarely had more than a few moments alone at any given time, day or night. Not that I knew and I didn't want to know.

Leaving Sarah's phone alone, I slipped out the front door. I paused a moment, hesitating to leave the door unlocked with her asleep inside. But there was literally no one else around. And if anyone came down the road, I would see them.

Deciding it would be okay, I took off at a slow jog heading toward the road. It was a country road, just wide enough for two cars. In Houston it could easily be a path through a park.

The sun was warm on my skin and as I moved into the familiar jog, my thoughts took the opportunity to wander.

They immediately found their way around to Zoe and last night's kisses.

I liked it that she seemed okay with taking things slowly, on the physical side, at least. So many girls would expect a guy to jump into bed with them.

I found her refreshing. And exhilarating at the same time.

I hadn't been able to stop thinking about her since I'd seen her standing at the Abilene airport, looking completely vexed.

It always made me smile to think about that.

I knew when the cell service kicked in. My phone chimed with messages. I stopped right there in the middle of the deserted road, beneath a grove of blooming jacaranda trees, and checked.

Nothing but a message from Aunt Madison checking on me. Making sure I was okay. I sent her a quick message back. Told her I was in an area with no cell service.

It was as good as sending a message to the whole family. Not that they were gossips, but we were close and, especially with this going on with Grandma, we were staying in touch with each other.

I ran another mile, then turned around and headed back. Oddly enough I didn't want to be away from Sarah.

Now that I'd found her, it was going to be hard to pry myself away from her.

Not that I wanted to. Not in the least.

I picked up speed as I headed back to the house, then slowed again the last few yards to start cooling off.

There was something sitting right in front of the front door. A box. A solid white box about the size of a man's shoebox. Tied with a red ribbon that looked more like twine when I got closer.

It had not been there when I had left. I couldn't have gotten out the door without walking right over it.

A tremor ran down my spine. I slowed to a walk, turning and scanning the area.

There was no way anyone could have come here while I was out without driving right past me.

Reaching the door, I picked up the box and, with one more glance behind me, took it inside with me. I set it on the table next to Sarah's phone.

Then I went in search of her. She wasn't in the parlor or the kitchen or in the study.

My heart pounding, I dashed upstairs, taking the steps, two at the time.

"Sarah," I said, pounding on her door and trying hard to resist barging in.

She came to the door, looking charmingly tousled, and looked curiously at me.

"What's wrong?" she asked.

I let out a slow breath. "I just needed to know that you're okay."

"I just got up. Why?"

"I went for a quick run and when I got back, there was a...

Billionaire's Unexpected Landing 193

package at the door. But nobody came down the road while I was out."

"A package?" she asked, turning pale. Pale with an almost green tint.

"A box."

"I need to see it," she said, slipping past me. She was still wearing her pajamas. Long gray sleep pants and a t-shirt. "Where?"

"I left it downstairs. In the foyer."

I followed her down the stairs and stood next to her as she stared at the box as though it might bite her.

I looked from her to the box and back again.

"What is it?" I asked.

When she looked at me, meeting my gaze, I saw those shadows again. And this time, I knew I hadn't put them there.

She picked up the little card from the flower shop and handed it to me.

"Read this," she said.

I pulled the card out of the envelope with her name printed on it.

Until next time.

"What does this mean?" I asked. "Who sent it?" I turned the card over, but there was no other name on it. Just the name of a flower shop in town. No sender.

Staring at the box again, she shook her head. "I don't know. It came two days ago with some red roses."

I looked around. "Where are they?"

"I returned them," she said.

"Returned them?" I asked, trying not to laugh. "How do you return flowers?"

She looked at me crossly. "I took them to the flower shop. But they wouldn't tell me who sent them."

The alarm shot along my spine again.

A little late, perhaps, but I locked the door and walked through the house again. The parlor, study, and kitchen. The other rooms were closed down, sheets over the furniture. Nonetheless, I made a quick walk through all the rooms, making sure there was no one here.

"Do you mind if I look upstairs?" I asked.

Sarah was alternating her gaze between me and the box.

"Do you want me to open it?" I asked when I got back downstairs, having found no sign of an intruder.

That seemed to nudge her out of her shock.

"I'll do it," she said.

I watched as she grabbed a pair of scissors from a little drawer under the table, snipped the red ribbon and opened the plain white box.

She pulled out a rectangular wooden box and with a quick glance at me, opened it.

The box was empty, but it immediately began playing a romantic musical tune.

She set it down again like it had burned her.

Reaching around her, I picked up the music box and examined it, looking for something to identify it, but there was nothing. Not even a card. There wasn't a card in the box either.

"Who is this from?" I asked, mostly to myself.

Her gaze met mine. "You're the only person who knows where I am," she said, with a wry smile.

"Well, it's not from me," I said. "If I was going to give you something I would just give it to you."

She nodded and I followed her into the parlor to sit on the sofa.

"Any idea who might be sending you gifts?" I asked.

She shook her head and looked blankly out the window.

Whoever it was, it most definitely had her disconcerted.

And it had all my protective instincts in high gear.

And it had me thinking how fortuitous it was that I was here.

There was no way I was going to let her out of my sight now. I knew more than I wanted to know about stalking and the dangers that came with it.

61

SARAH

I stood beneath the hot water in the shower, letting the warmth wash away the chill that had come over me at the sight of the unexpected box.

The flowers had come by delivery through a flower shop, so that was one thing.

But this box had been dropped off at my doorstep not even a full two days later. And on top of that, it had been dropped off right under Luke's nose. He had been *outside* jogging when it had been dropped off.

How?

How had someone dropped off a package without him seeing them?

There was one road in and one road out. No neighbors less than a mile away.

It just wasn't physically possible.

Someone had gone to far too much nefarious dealings for my comfort.

And damn it. It made my blood boil.

I wanted to think about Luke. Not some stalker.

The word froze my thoughts.

Did I really have a stalker?

I didn't have an ex-boyfriend who would be stalking me. And I hadn't even turned anyone down for a date lately.

What was I supposed to do with this?

It wasn't police worthy. They'd probably laugh at me. *Why are you complaining about someone sending flowers?* Just like the woman at the flower shop who had thought it was romantic.

Although the flowers had been disconcerting, I think I could have gotten past that—if it had only been that. But now it was a music box, too.

And it wasn't just the music box. If it had come in the mail it would have one thing, but being dropped off like that was just plain creepy.

I turned off the water and grabbed a towel.

I was not going to let this ruin my time with Luke.

That's what a stalker would want. Didn't they want attention?

Well, I wasn't going to give whoever it was any attention. And if I didn't need the music box for evidence I'd take it out back and burn it.

I also hated that Luke was the only candidate. The only person who knew where I was.

I turned on the hair dryer and forced myself to think about something else.

Luke.

That was a much more pleasant line of thinking.

I was glad he was here. For so many reasons.

I felt safer, but I also liked him. I liked him more and more by the hour, it seemed.

Maybe we needed to get out of here today.

Sitting around here feeling nervous that someone might be watching—and how could they not be watching to have known when to drop off the box—was not how I wanted to spend my time.

Determined not to let this ruin my day, I put on a flowy white skirt and a little t-shirt, topped off by a little burgundy leather jacket.

I'd brought nice clothes. It was too ingrained in me not to. I might not have brought much food, but I never traveled anywhere without appropriate clothes for just about any occasion. I had not brought a dress for a black-tie event, but I had brought clothes for just about anything else.

Dressed for the day, I went downstairs to find Luke standing looking out one of the parlor windows, his hands behind his back.

"Hi," I said, with what I hoped was a bright smile.

"Hi," he turned. He, too, had showered and dressed for the day. He was wearing jeans and a blue oxford shirt, freshly shaved with hair still damp on the ends.

I didn't fight it when my heart turned a flip. I just enjoyed the sensation, letting it sweep over me.

"Feel better?" he asked, walking toward me, taking me in his arms.

"Much better," I said. "How do you feel about getting out of here?"

62

LUKE

Freshly showered, Sarah smelled like a swirl of honeysuckle and maybe lilac. Whatever it was, it was lovely and just faint enough to be tantalizing.

I had been a bit worried about her when she'd headed upstairs, but now she seemed to have gotten over the shock of finding a music box on the doorstep. A second gift from an unknown and obviously unwanted admirer.

I wanted to talk to her more about who could be stalking her, but not wanting to be the one to remind her of it, I didn't say anything.

We took my car. No reason in particular. I just happened to have my keys out.

I set my phone on the little mid-dash console with an automatic charger and she set hers beside mine. Our phones, both with black cases, were identical.

Right on cue, about a mile down the road just as we passed the grove of spectacular blooming jacaranda trees, our cell phones came to life.

Since I was driving, I had to wait to check mine, but I just checked this morning anyway.

Sarah, who hadn't checked her messages since sometime yesterday, grabbed her cell up.

A couple of minutes later, she set it back on the charger.

"Anything?" I asked.

"A message from Mr. Madris."

"About the job?" I asked. "What did he say?"

"I'll listen to it later," she said with a little shrug.

I looked at her sideways. "You can wait like that?"

"I don't want to know yet," she said, smiling over at me.

"Why not?"

"Because then I have to start thinking about choices," she said. "And I just want to enjoy the day." She swept a hand in the general direction of the passenger window.

That actually made sense in an unexpected way. I wasn't sure I could have waited, but I had always known what I wanted to be and where I would work. I'd never had a life-changing decision like that to make. I'd always known I would live in Houston and work for Skye Travels.

"So all this was your winery?" I asked as we drove through fields of vines.

"Yep," she said. "It's just as well. I'm a city girl and my father, well… he would never have done anything with it. It would have just been sitting there, lying fallow as they say."

"That wouldn't be good," I said. Though I knew nothing about vineyards, I knew that lying fallow could not be a good thing.

She laughed and I felt her looking at me. "I'm really glad you're here," she said.

"Me too," I said.

A little later we made it to town and parked on the side of the street near the café.

We walked hand-in-hand along the sidewalk to the café doors.

Billionaire's Unexpected Landing   201

The hostess led us through the building to the back of the café to a charming little outdoor courtyard.

There were a dozen tables, half of them occupied. A light-colored stone wall surrounded the courtyard on three sides, the only opening a little iron gate.

Deep green ivies climbed along the stone wall, giving the wall depth and making it look like it had been here forever.

The table was covered with a white tablecloth and four empty wine glasses upside down. The hostess took two of the wine glasses away.

I held one of the chairs for Sarah, then sat next to her.

"What's good here?" I asked, picking up one of the single page menus.

"I have no idea," she said, glancing over at me. "The last time I was here was... years ago."

Deciding I'd just have what she had, I set the menu aside and watched her instead.

63

SARAH

*I*t was hard to concentrate with Luke watching me.

I quickly picked out something that would suit my taste and let my thoughts wander a moment while keeping my gaze on the menu.

I really was glad that Luke was here.

When we'd walked in, I had quickly scanned the other tables, looking for someone, anyone, who looked familiar... or threatening.

There were several couples, a couple of older couples, a young couple, and a mother and daughter. No one who looked the least bit threatening... or familiar.

I hated that whoever had sent me flowers and then dropped off a music box had me being hypervigilant.

I also hated that they had my brain trying to solve the puzzle. How could someone have gotten the box to the door without Luke seeing them?

And most of all, I hated the trace of a possibility that Luke had been the one to send the flowers and that the box was from him.

Billionaire's Unexpected Landing   203

That's what bothered me the most right now. I hated that they had me doubting Luke in the least. Because I didn't.

I set my menu aside and met his gaze.

The way he looked at me made my breath hitch.

The server interrupted the moment by bringing a bottle of wine to the table.

"Compliments of the house," she said.

I glanced at Luke and fought the urge to look over my shoulder. He must have had a similar concern that the wine had been sent by someone else... the stalker.

"Thank you," he said, his voice calm. "Is this customary?"

"Yes," she said, leaning forward and lowering her voice. "If you like it, you can buy a bottle."

"Which winery?" I asked, with relief.

"Garrison Valley Winery," she said as she poured wine in my glass. "It used to be Lawrence Valley Winery, but they sold out years ago."

I just nodded.

After she left, Luke and I tasted the wine.

"Not bad," he said.

"It actually tastes a little bit familiar," I said.

"It must be hard," he said. "Being here and seeing what could have been."

I shook my head and twirled the glass by the stem. "I'm glad they're doing well. It was never my dream to live out here. To farm the land."

"Mine either," he said.

"You like to be in the sky," I said, enjoying the change of conversation.

"At the age when most parents are teaching their babies to swim, my grandfather had me in an airplane."

"Is that even legal?" I asked.

Luke laughed. "I don't know. Probably not. But I've never

known anyone to tell Noah Worthington he couldn't do something."

"Are you the oldest grandchild?"

"No," he said, after a moment's consideration. "I think we all got a turn."

"So that's why you became a pilot?"

"I guess it's in my blood."

"It must be nice," I said. "To have such a big family."

"I've never known anything else," he said.

"Do you—?" I stopped myself. I was going to ask him if he wanted a large family, but my phone was ringing.

"It's my boss, Zachary," I said.

"You should take it."

64

LUKE

I was learning that Sarah didn't like to answer her cell phone. Or even listen to her messages.

I didn't have that luxury. If someone called, I had to answer or I could miss out on something important regarding a flight change or a passenger.

Today was different though. We weren't at work. I liked that she could separate the two.

After lunch as we sat and finished our glass of wine, I sent my grandmother a text.

ME: *Are you feeling well?*

A minute or so later, she sent back a message.

GRANDMA SAVANNAH: *Hello Luke. I feel quite well. Your grandfather won't let me out of his sight. He won't let me eat anything that is not boringly healthy.*

ME: *Good. Make sure he pampers you.*

GRANDMA SAVANNAH: *I have no choice.*

I knew that her complaints weren't real. Grandma and Grandpa loved each other more than anything.

ME: *I'm headed back to an area without cell phone service.*

"I envy you," Sarah said.

"Some people would think we're too much into each other's business."

"They're just jealous," she said, staring at her own cell phone.

Most everyone else had left the café and the only other diners were across the room.

Sarah put her phone on speaker and listened to the message from Mr. Madris.

"Hello Sarah. This is Mr. Madris. I'm calling to let you know that in light of everything that's going on, I'm not able to offer you the job."

Sarah just looked at me, her eyes wide with confusion.

I didn't know him very well, but it sounded strangely cryptic to me.

"What's that supposed to mean?" I asked.

"I didn't get the job," she said.

"Maybe you should call him back," I said. "Find out why."

She shook her head with a little smile.

"I didn't think I would. The other candidate, Tyler, lives in Houston. They already know him and they don't have to move him."

"Huh." I would have been on the phone. Asking for an explanation. But maybe Sarah was okay with it. Maybe she didn't really want the job. It would have been a huge move for her. Moving from California to Houston.

It would have taken her from her world.

Besides, it wasn't my business.

"Everything happens the way it's supposed to," I said, quoting my grandmother. Anytime something like this happened, that was her explanation.

I knew that her life had taken a lot of unexpected turns and twists and yet she had landed on right where she needed to be.

"I know," Sarah said, straightening and putting on a brave face. "Something else will come along."

Billionaire's Unexpected Landing   207

I took her hand and kissed the back of her fingers. I felt a strong need to distract her.

"Want to walk around? Check out the shops?"

"Sounds good," she said.

As we headed out of the café, I wrestled with my own disappointment that I hadn't wanted her to see.

I'd been selfishly hoping she would get the job in Houston. I wanted her to move to Houston so we could see each other every day.

Now that wasn't going to happen and I realized she was right.

Listening to that message had me thinking about choices.

Now I had to figure out something. Even if it was a long-distance relationship.

65

SARAH

*M*y emotions were all over the place as we drove back to the house.

I tried hard to hide my disappointment at not getting the job in Houston. I wanted the job or at least the option of taking the job. At one time it had been about the job itself, but somehow it had become more about moving to be closer to Luke than the job itself.

When I thought about it, I knew that I liked my job here on the west coast. I could ask for less travel, but I liked the physicians I worked with.

Luke and I didn't talk much as we rode back to the house. We'd visited a couple of shops—a wine shop, a trinket store, and an antique store.

We also stopped at the market to pick up food to cook tonight.

I'd enjoyed the afternoon with Luke.

But it was bittersweet. I would be going back to work soon, as would he.

I tried to focus on the moment.

But as the road narrowed and we got closer to the house, I

Billionaire's Unexpected Landing 209

found myself again trying to figure out how someone could have gotten that box to the door when Luke was out jogging. He said he'd only gone out a couple of miles. Maybe less.

It was less because he'd turned around before he reached the neighbor's house.

When the flowers came, I'd been disconcerted, but I'd imagined the sender being somewhere else not here.

Now I was looking around every tree. Watching every shadow, even though I tried not to.

It was a lot of work fighting back the paranoia and the anger that came with it. I didn't like being a victim.

I didn't understand it. Who would want to frighten me like this? Maybe they thought they were doing something nice.

I shoved the hair out of my face and let out a sigh.

"Want to talk about it?" Luke asked.

"It's just the unwanted gifts," I admitted. "I can't stop trying to figure it all out. Is it a stalker?"

He looked over at me sideways. There was something in his expression that I did not like.

"It sounds like a stalker," he said.

I looked away. "I just don't want it to be."

"Have you gotten any texts or phone calls?"

"No." I knew what he meant. Stalkers usually did more than just send gifts.

"Has anyone been showing up, seemingly randomly at places where you are?"

"Just you," I said, with a little smile.

He grimaced. "I'm going to have to start being more careful. You're on to me."

"I am," I said. "But shouldn't you be trying to contact me?"

"Why would I contact you when I can talk to you in person?"

"Good point." I waited a beat. "How do you know so much about stalkers?"

"My Aunt Brianna had a stalker once."

My eyes widened. "Brianna Worthington is your aunt? I watch her YouTube channel."

"Along with thousands of other people," he said. "And one of them is now in prison."

"Oh my God. Did he hurt her?"

"Not physically, no. But she's more careful now than she was. And her husband watches her like a hawk."

"I bet. She's lucky to have him."

"He and Grandpa went after him."

I stared out the window as we passed the jacaranda trees.

"Is this how it started?" I asked. "With gifts?"

"Sort of," he said. "If I remember correctly, the first thing he did was to send flowers. Anonymously."

I sat back and closed my eyes. This was not what I wanted to hear.

But I needed to hear it. I needed to know. And I needed to be careful.

I decided right then and there that when Luke left, I was leaving, too. I was not going to stay out by myself.

66

LUKE

*A*fter a steak dinner, I lit a fire in the fireplace to chase away the evening chill.

Sarah and I settled into the parlor, on opposite ends of the sofa, our feet—both wearing white socks—meeting in the middle.

Our day had been good. Spending some time in town had been a good idea. And there were no presents at the door when we got home.

I hoped that my being here discouraged whoever was trying to get Sarah's attention through unwanted gifts. Even though I hoped it, I knew it didn't work that way. Aunt Brianna had been happily married when she was stalked.

It had not done one lick of good. But a man had to have hope.

We had the letters from Rebecca and Nathaniel ready to read.

"Who's turn is it?" I asked, though I knew perfectly well that it was her turn.

"It's mine," she said, picking up the letter on top.

"My dearest Nathaniel."

She looked up at me. "She's becoming more affectionate with him."

"I see that," I said. "But he started it."

She laughed. "You're right. He did."

She went on to read an accounting of Rebecca's week. She had traveled into town to visit her cousins. The first time she had traveled since before Nathaniel had left.

"Yours truly, Rebecca."

She set down the paper and looked at me. "Your turn."

I picked up the next letter. This one was not so worn. Obviously a letter that Rebecca had kept.

"My dearest Rebecca." I glanced up at Sarah. She leaned her cheek against the back of the sofa and smiled.

My God she was beautiful. If I hadn't thought it would freak her out, I would have gotten up just to grab my cell phone to take a picture of her.

"I've had a lot of time to think. And now that I've seen battle, I'm looking at things differently. Thinking about what I want. How I want my life to be."

I read a little more. Then stopped. "It looked like he stopped and came back the next day."

"Okay," Sarah said, clearly relaxed.

I thought about setting the letter aside and joining her on her side of the sofa, but I really did want to know what Nathaniel was going to say next.

"He's coming home," I said.

"Hey," she said, straightening. "No skipping ahead."

"I'm not skipping ahead," I said, but I knew I was guilty.

I'm coming home, but I only have two days before I return. Will —" I stopped and looked up at Sarah. I was skipping ahead again.

"Will you marry me?" Those were the next words on the page, but I wasn't looking at the paper. I didn't have to.

Nathaniel had just proposed to Rebecca. By letter.

After they had only known each other for two days.

I set the paper aside and sat up, moving toward Sarah.

I pulled her into my arms and pressed my lips to hers.

The words I had just said out loud reverberated through my head.

And the odd thing was, they felt right.

Nathaniel's words rang true.

67

SARAH

The fire crackled in the fireplace, sending out little sparks that landed on the hearth inside the screen.

Luke had bought two bundles of firewood and we'd already burned up one. It was relaxing sitting in front of the fire. It didn't matter that it was barely cool enough to even have a fire in the first place.

It hadn't mattered that I had already read the letters through once. It was a completely different experience going through them with Luke. Reading the words my ancestors had written each other when they had been young and in love.

It didn't matter that I knew Nathaniel had proposed to Sarah by letter.

I know she married him eventually, but I don't know if she married him on his two day leave or not. This was the last letter in that box.

When Luke had read that proposal out loud, he had been looking at me. Either he had said it like he meant it or I had heard it like he meant it.

Either way, my heart was practically beating out of my chest.

Yes. I wanted to say yes.

But it wasn't really a question.

It was a letter.

So I lost myself in his kisses. Focused on the moment. On Luke being right here. Right now.

His kisses spoke of promises. Gentle. Hungry. And I matched him kiss for kiss. Giving him unspoken promises right back.

"I need some water," I said, a few minutes later.

"I'll get it," Luke said.

"No. It's okay." I stood up and squeezed his hand. I just needed a minute. Just a minute to clear my head before I started believing that Luke had really proposed to me.

He hadn't. He'd merely been reading Nathaniel's letter. A letter I had already read. But the words sounded so much different coming from his lips.

As I stood at the kitchen window and drank a bottle of water that Luke had bought in town, I realized my hands were shaking.

I also realized that I was falling hard for him.

I liked everything about him. His gorgeous blue eyes. The way he smelled like cedar and soap. His kissable lips.

Now that I had admitted it to myself, I felt better. More steady and relaxed.

Feeling happier than I could remember feeling in a long time, I headed back out to the parlor where Luke was waiting.

Since there was no cell phone service here, we both kept our phones plugged in on the little table in the foyer.

On my way by, out of habit, I touched my phone's screen. Just in case.

And froze.

I had a message. It must have come in just as we were driving up to the house and somehow I hadn't seen it.

I picked up the phone and touched the screen again.

FATHER: *You need to come home.*

My heart lodged in my throat. What had happened? What was wrong?

But there was another message beneath it. I slid it up so I could read it.

FATHER: *You need to know. Zoe is pregnant.*

About a hundred thoughts collided in my head.

My father's name was listed under Dad in my phone.

This was not my phone.

Zoe was pregnant.

I dropped the phone back on the table. The messages must have come in just as we got back and Luke had not seen them.

Luke came to the door.

"Are you okay?"

I looked at him, not bothering to hide the pain and shock that I know must be all over my face.

Whirling around, I ran up the stairs.

"Sarah!"

Luke called after me, but I wanted nothing to do with him.

Reaching my room, I locked the door behind me, and leaned against the cool wood.

"Sarah, what's wrong? What's happened?" Luke called from the other side of the door.

Ignoring him, I walked to the bed and fell onto it.

Then I just let my mind go blank.

68

LUKE

I sat in the parlor and tried to figure out what had happened to make Sarah look at me like that. Like I'd broken her heart. Then she had run away from me. She'd locked me out of her bedroom.

I watched the last of the wood as it burned down to embers and replayed our day. Our night.

What could possibly have tripped in her head from the time I was reading the letter, then kissing her?

That's when she had gotten up to get some water.

I could still feel her lips on mine.

I picked up Nathaniel's letter and reread it.

Will you marry me?

That had to be it.

Either I was the last person in the world that she wanted to marry or the question had triggered something deep and traumatic.

Either way, there was nothing I could do about it right now.

After making sure the fire was banked, I headed up to my room.

Whatever it was, it would look better in the morning.

I opened the window and let the cool air settle me.

When I'd read Nathaniel's words, they had felt so real. I honestly felt like I was really proposing to her.

I'd never proposed to anyone before.

How was it that it seemed so real?

Was it because we'd read the letters Nathaniel and Rebecca had written each other all those years ago, building up to the same feelings they had built up to?

I wondered if Rebecca had answered him.

She obviously had said yes. They were Sarah's great-great-grandparents. But had she married him during his two-day furlough? Or sometime later?

Sarah probably didn't even have an answer to that.

If I had Internet I'd do some research and see if I could find out.

That would be something Sarah might like to know.

And that brought me back around to her stalker.

I hadn't wanted to frighten her, but Aunt Brianna's stalker had started off almost identical to this. And he had escalated to the point of physically showing up at her house.

And she was even already married to Uncle Jackson.

I didn't know the details, because I had been a child when it happened, but the boldness of the guy never ceased to amaze me.

He was in prison now, but that didn't keep some other guy from doing the same thing to Sarah.

I was not a violent person, but growing with four brothers, I knew how to hold my own.

If Sarah's stalker showed up here and tried to hurt her, he wouldn't be leaving in one piece.

That was one thing I was certain of.

69

SARAH

*T*he drive back to L.A. was one of the worst drives of my entire life.

I'd gotten up before daylight, packed all my things, and left the country house.

It probably wasn't the smartest thing I had ever done, leaving Luke in my own house.

I frankly had not cared if he locked it up or not. All I knew was that I could not face him.

I felt like I had been turned inside out.

The man I was falling for had gotten another girl pregnant. A girl he claimed he didn't even know other than in passing.

How had he lied to me like that? The lie had just rolled off his tongue smooth as silk.

It made me question everything.

Maybe he was even my stalker.

I shuddered at the thought as I pulled into the garage of my townhouse.

I'd trusted him. I'd let him spend the night in my home— technically my father's home—and he was nothing more than a liar.

If I cared about someone, I could tolerate a lot. Bad moods. Forgotten dates. But lying.

That was a whole different level. That was something I could not tolerate.

A relationship was based on trust at the very core and without it, there was nothing. Nothing to build on. No foundation that could last.

I felt utterly stupid.

Rules were there for a reason. *Don't date out of town.*

I'd always followed that rule.

I had served me well.

And it was a rule I would never be caught breaking again.

A quick look in the mirror told me I looked like hell. My eyes were puffy and swollen from crying and my hair looked like something akin to a rat's nest.

I stood beneath the hot water in the shower until it ran cool. It helped a little bit to wash off the past few days.

Still feeling out of sorts and needing to distract myself, I ordered Chinese food and sat down at my computer to answer all the emails I had missed the past few days.

Nothing important except that Zachary had called a meeting for one o'clock today. A mandatory meeting. Apparently something urgent had come up.

Just as the doorbell rang with my lunch delivery, I got a text.

I stopped halfway down the stairs to check the message.

ZACHARY: *I hope you're back. We have a meeting today at 1:00. It's mandatory.*

I rolled my eyes.

ME: *Just got home. I'll be there.*

I needed to put on makeup and decent clothes. It would be good to feel back to normal. Time off was sorely overrated. All it did for me was to make me feel out of sorts.

Billionaire's Unexpected Landing 221

I opened the door, expecting to see the little delivery guy who always brought my food.

Instead, I saw…

I blinked.

Surely not.

70

LUKE

I stood in Sarah's bedroom, unable to make sense of anything.

I'd gotten up that morning, showered, then made myself some toast and coffee.

I'd waited until seven o'clock before I went searching for Sarah. It was nine o'clock in Houston and I felt like I'd been up all day.

Surprised and alarmed to find her bedroom door standing open, I stood in the doorway, making a quick assessment.

She wasn't there.

It didn't take long to figure out that her things were gone, too.

I ran my hands through my hair.

Surely not. Surely she hadn't left.

Then I went to the window and looked down.

Her car was gone.

Good God.

I hadn't been out back all day or I would have already known she wasn't here.

Maybe something had happened.

Billionaire's Unexpected Landing   223

The only family she had was her father.

Something must have happened with her father.

Why didn't she wake me?

I would have gone with her. Wherever she had to go.

I took off downstairs to call her. No cell service, but I'd drive down to the trees, call her, then come back and lock up the house.

I wasn't sure how I felt about that. I was a little offended that she hadn't gotten me up or at least left me a note. Maybe she'd been too upset to even think about doing something like that. But either way, I was honored that she had trusted me to lock up the house.

I grabbed my keys, then my phone.

There was a message on my phone.

Thinking it might be from Sarah... stranger things had happened, I unlocked the screen.

FATHER: *You need to come home.*

FATHER: *You need to know. Zoe is pregnant.*

First of all, why was Father sending me this? He knew I was in California and didn't have cell phone service.

Second, why was it he thought that Zoe being pregnant had anything to do with me?

Well hell.

I might as well lock up and head out. Knowing this house wasn't used much, I knew there was a lot to do.

I cleaned out the fireplace, emptied out the refrigerator, and covered up the furniture.

My mind racing, I worked quickly.

Now that I knew Sarah wasn't here, I felt a sense of urgency.

Before leaving, I carefully folded up the letters between Nathaniel and Rebecca and put them back in their box. I almost brought them with me, but they weren't mine to bring.

When I got to the blooming jacaranda trees, my phone

populated with new messages. I'd never know why father's messages made it through and none of the others did.

With a sense of impending doom, I pulled over and my hands trembled as I opened the text from Sarah.

SARAH: *At home. Gift. Help.*

My gut flipped over on itself and tried to send me into a tailspin.

But I took a deep breath.

For whatever reason, Sarah had gone home. L.A. She lived in L.A.

I got back on the road, driving like a madman.

The stalker must have followed her there. And she was in trouble.

There were a lot of things that didn't make sense to me, but right now it didn't matter.

Right now all that mattered was that I get help to Sarah.

But I didn't know who to call. I didn't even know her address.

I did the only thing I knew to do.

I called Grandpa.

71

SARAH

*A*t first I didn't recognize him.

I'd never seen Jeremy outside of Dr. Meek's office.

"Jeremy?" I asked, looking over his shoulder.

Surely there was a mistake. Where was the Chinese guy who always brought my deliveries?

"Hi Sarah," Jeremy said.

Wearing jeans and a polo shirt, he looked like a completely different person.

I fought to put everything together.

"Why are you here? Why aren't you at work?" How did he even know where to find me?

"I took the week off," he said with a grin.

But really. Why was he here at my home? I'd never even had a personal conversation with him.

I'd talked to him about medicine a couple of times at Dr. Meek's office, but only business.

How? Why? He was here. At my home.

Something was wrong. Very wrong.

"I'm just leaving," I said. "I have a meeting at the office."

Then he held up his hands and it registered that he was holding my Chinese takeout bag.

"If you're leaving, why did you just order lunch?"

"I'm taking it with me," I said, slamming the door, leaving him holding the bag of food.

But his foot was in the door.

"You forgot your food," he said, so calmly. As though this were a normal conversation.

"I don't have time for it now," I said. "You keep it."

"Eat with me," he said. "Before you go."

"Move. Your. Foot." I said, pushing as hard as I could against the door.

But he was stronger than I was and he was pushing back.

Seconds later, he was standing inside my condo.

Uninvited.

"What do you want?" I asked, holding my hands together to give me strength.

"I just want to spend time with you."

Everything flashed together.

The flowers. The music box. The conversation with Luke about his Aunt Brianna.

And I just knew.

Jeremy was my stalker.

I forced a smile on my face. And he smiled back.

Just play along. Don't let him think anything is wrong.

"I have to let my boss know that I'm going to be late. I just need to send him a quick message."

Watching him carefully, I pulled my phone out of my back pocket.

Zachary wouldn't understand. He didn't know anything about what was going on.

I went with my gut.

ME: *At home. Gift. Help.*

"Give me your phone," Jeremy said.

I hit send.

And then his fingers were biting into my upper arm as he led me to my dining room. My own dining room.

"Why are you here?"

His only answer was to grab my phone out of my hands and toss it across the room.

"You won't be needing this. It's just us now." He put the bag of food down when we reached the table and pulled out a chair.

Then he sat next to me.

"This is nice," he said. "Just the two of us now."

"Jeremy," I said. "What's wrong with you? What are you doing here?"

He looked at me with such malice, confirming my first response to just play along with whatever he wanted.

"I'll get some plates," I said.

He put a hand on my arm again. I was going to have bruises. Good. I needed proof.

Then I remembered that I had a security camera on my front door. All I had to do was to stay alive.

72

LUKE

The drive from the vineyard was one of the longest trips I'd ever made.

Grandpa knew what to do.

"Just drive safely," he said. "Don't worry. Let me take care of it."

Don't worry.

That would be like telling him not to worry about Grandma Savannah.

But Noah had all the contacts. He would call Mr. Madris…

My gut wrenched.

Mr. Madris might not be talking to us Worthingtons.

If his granddaughter was pregnant and she was pointing a finger toward us… that was a move as old as time. But DNA would tell the tale.

Men were no longer trapped like they used to be.

They could find out whether or not a child was theirs.

I knew it certainly wasn't mine.

And with Zoe being pregnant, hopefully that took the attention away from me and put it where it belonged. On the father.

Billionaire's Unexpected Landing   **229**

Good God. With all of Zoe's guy friends, the list of suspects was long.

All I knew and all I cared about was that it was not me.

I pounded my hands on the steering wheel. I had no way to contact Sarah's office in L.A.

I had to count on Grandpa to get through to whoever he needed to get to so he could get help to Sarah.

I kept an eye on the phone in case Sarah called back, but I didn't contact her.

If the stalker was with her, I didn't want to do anything that would make things worse for her.

I pulled onto the interstate and floored it. I passed other cars like they were sitting still. I only cared about a speeding ticket because it would slow me down.

Flying was so much more efficient. And there was no speed limit.

But unfortunately cars did not fly. Yet.

I was going to be first in line when flying cars came out.

Didn't have a care about self-driving cars. Just give me one that would lift off the ground and fly.

As I drove, my brain caught up with my gut.

It was Sarah.

Sarah was the one for me.

I was going to marry her.

I'd never felt this way about another woman.

I suddenly understood my father who waited forever, forsaking all others for years while he searched for a girl he had met at some kind of conference.

He'd waited. He'd known who he wanted.

That's what I would be doing.

I knew who I wanted. And I would wait.

Whatever had bothered Sarah enough last night that she had left without telling me, we had to work it out.

Whatever it was, we would fix it.

All I had to do was to keep her alive.

And then I was going to marry her.

Of course, the only other thing I had to do was to convince her.

This drive was taking too long and once I reached L.A. I didn't know where to go. I called Grandpa, but he didn't answer his phone.

I called Father, but he didn't answer either.

I couldn't just do nothing.

"Hey Siri," I said. "Call the Los Angeles police department."

"The only option I found is Los Angeles police department on West First Street in Los Angeles. Would you like me to call it?"

"Yes," I said, squeezing the steering wheel and gritting my teeth.

Someone came on the line.

"I need your help," I said.

"My name is Lucy. How can I help you, Sir?" The woman had no compassion in her voice. This was most definitely not Houston.

"My girlfriend is in danger," I said.

"What's the address?" she asked, still no compassion.

Address. "I don't know. Her name is Sarah Lawrence."

"Do you have the address where we need to send responders?"

"She's at her home," I said.

"What's the address, Sir?" she asked.

"I. Don't. Know." I needed to stay calm. "Just look it up. Her name is Sarah Lawrence. She works at Clinical Pharm."

"What is your name, Sir," she asked.

"Luke Worthington," I said.

"Your address?"

I gave her my address.

Lucy was quiet a moment. I felt an inkling of hope.

Billionaire's Unexpected Landing   231

"I can't just look up a person's address," she said. "without just cause."

"Lucy," I said. "Her life is in danger."

"How do you know this, Sir?"

"She sent me a text."

"Is she injured?"

"I don't know."

But that apparently was the wrong thing to say.

"Please call back when you have more information."

"No."

But Lucy disconnected the call.

No. Don't hang up.

What kind of place was L.A. that a person could not even get help?

This was not someplace I would ever want to live.

Then I did what I'd told myself I wouldn't do.

I called Sarah.

73

SARAH

$\mathcal{I}$ would never eat Chinese food again. It tasted like cardboard and it smelled rank. Like nothing anyone would want to put in their mouth.

And to think that I used to like Chinese food.

But I pretended to eat.

Pretended to be having a pleasant lunch with Jeremy.

Psycho Jeremy.

I never would have known he was a stalker. That he was unhinged. The only indication had been that last day at Dr. Meek's office when he'd tried to block my path. But it seemed innocent.

It had seemed a little flirty, even. But that was something I was used to. Doctors and interns tended to do that. It didn't faze me. I had actually learned to use it to my advantage.

I little flirting helped when I was working with guys. That's why Zachary sent me. I knew how to flirt just enough to skirt the line and still make them want to listen to me. To consider using my medications.

It was an art.

And I had thought I had it perfected.

Jeremy wasn't looking at me. He was concentrating on eating.

The bastard owed me a lunch.

When my phone began to ring, Jeremy looked at me sharply.

He slid his chair back and located my phone on the other side of the room.

He owed me a cell phone, too.

"Luke Worthington," he said, then added tauntingly. "Is that someone you want to talk to?"

"No," I lied. "I don't care about him."

Jeremy grinned. How had I ever thought he was the least bit attractive?

The phone went silent.

"Why don't we send him a little message?" he asked.

I shook my head. "No. Let's don't."

Jeremy held the phone in front of my face, but I turned away.

He grabbed my chin and held my face steady until my phone unlocked.

I was going to be sick.

"What's this?" he asked, kicking a back leg of my chair.

"I don't know."

"Help? You lied to me. You told me you were going to write Zachary."

I really was going to be sick. He knew my boss's name.

"I don't tolerate lying," he said.

Yeah. Me either. Nor do I tolerate psychos forcing their way into my home.

He was typing on my phone.

"What are you doing?" I asked, feeling sick.

"Luke Worthington won't be bothering you anymore. You don't have to worry."

"What—?"

The palm of his hand slapping across my cheek, stopped anything I was going to say.

"You've had enough to eat," he said. "Can't have you getting fat."

He grabbed me by the arm.

"We'll sit in the living room now and have a little chat."

74

LUKE

*S*ARAH: *Do not contact me again. I have found my one true love.*

My stomach clenched as I read the latest message from Sarah.

Then I took a deep breath. That didn't sound like her. It was too stilted. It was not from her.

It simply told me that she was in even more trouble.

I was on the outskirts of L.A. and I had no idea where to go from here. Which direction did I need to go? I couldn't just drive around L.A. with no direction and expect to find Sarah's house.

"Hey Siri. Call Grandpa."

He didn't answer.

I was starting to panic.

"Hey Siri."

"Uh huh."

"Call Clinical Pharm."

"One option is Clinical Pharm on Westbrook drive. Is that the one you want?"

"Yes." *I don't know.*

I waited for someone to answer.

Then Grandpa beeped in. I hung up on Clinical Pharm and answered Grandpa's call.

"Luke," he said. "I haven't been able to reach Mr. Madris. I think he's avoiding my calls."

I was going to be sick. That was exactly what I was afraid of.

"Grandpa. I really, really think she's in danger. And I don't have any idea where she lives."

Grandpa was silent for a moment.

"Hold tight," he said and disconnected.

Hold tight. How was I supposed to hold tight driving with no destination down the freeway with my girlfriend's life in mortal danger?

I wasn't going to make the mistake of texting Sarah again.

Actually.... I moved over to the exit lane and got off the freeway.

I pulled over to the nearest gas station and stopped.

I googled Sarah's name.

She was one of about fifteen Sarah Lawrences in Los Angeles.

And I didn't see her photo attached to any of them.

How had a stalker found someone as private as Sarah?

Work.

That had to be the link.

Someone from her work was stalking her.

I got on the phone with Clinical Pharm again.

I was going to find her and when I did, someone was going to have hell to pay.

No psycho was going to get away from harming so much as a hair on her head, not to mention the emotional damage that came with it.

Billionaire's Unexpected Landing 237

Hell, I'd probably never be able to send her flowers without her remembering those flowers that been delivered anonymously to her.

I got transferred three time and by then I'd worked up a good mad.

75

SARAH

"After we're married, you won't have to work anymore," Jeremy said.

I think I just threw up in my mouth, but I put a smile on my face.

Psychotic, I decided. Definitely delusional.

Did he seriously entertain the idea that I would marry him? After he pushed his way into my home, dragged me by the arm to my own kitchen, and threw my phone across the room.

I'd never seen a psychotic person up close. I knew all about the medications that would treat him, but now I was seeing an up close and personal version of psychosis.

I needed my phone. I needed to call 911.

I'd texted Luke, but I didn't know if he would get the message. He was at my country home.

With no cell service.

I had wasted my one chance to contact someone. I should have dialed 911 instead.

I really was going to be late for my meeting with Zachary. I was never late for meetings. I was never late for anything. But

Zachary would chalk it up to me being upset about not getting the job in Houston.

He would have no reason to think about me needing help.

The little clock over my mantle chimed one time.

One o'clock.

I should be there.

Jeremy was still talking.

Five minutes later, my phone rang again.

"I should answer that," I said. "People are going to start worrying about me."

Quiet now, Jeremy just looked at me. The minutes ticked past.

"We need to write your resignation letter. Go ahead and send it in. Then we can put this place up for sale. I have a much nicer place for us. And our children."

I needed to get away from him. As far away as humanly possible.

"I have to go to the bathroom."

Jeremy was looking at me sideways. I don't think he believed me.

But I really did. And then I was going to be sick.

If I could just get out of his sight, I could get out of here.

I'd left Luke in my own country home this morning and I *liked* him. It was such irony that I needed to get away from my own condo now and couldn't.

I should have given Luke a chance to explain.

It was never a good idea to read someone else's messages out of context.

Even if Zoe was having his baby, it didn't mean he wanted to be with her.

And, not to be ugly, but from the guys following her around, there a possibility that the baby did not even belong to Luke.

Jeremy grabbed my arm, already sore, and pulled me to my

feet. He escorted—a new meaning of the word—me to the little half bath beneath my stairs and pushed me inside.

I turned the lock on the door.

Ha. I had gotten away from him.

But it only took a couple of minutes for me to figure out that this wasn't a solution to my problem.

But while I was here, I washed my hands and ran cold water over my face. It was a respite, if nothing else.

"Hurry up," Jeremy said through the door.

I ignored him.

He couldn't touch me in here.

It was quiet for five minutes, then I saw the doorknob move.

I stood back and watched.

Then the door open.

Jeremy stood there, proudly holding up a tiny little pick like something someone would use to work on their glasses.

How was it he just happened to have that with him? Because it most certainly was not mine.

He took me by the wrist this time and pulled out of the bathroom.

"We're going to write that letter now."

He pulled me along to the stairs, then started up them. I had not resisted him yet. Not since he'd slapped me.

For just a second, I felt his fingers loosen on mine. Just a little.

I tugged my hand loose and turned around, running.

I only got around three steps before he grabbed my hair.

Then everything went dark.

76

LUKE

Everything came together at the same time.

I got a text from Grandpa giving me Sarah's address at the same time I managed to convince Zachary that she was in danger enough that he sent me Sarah's address.

Apparently, Grandpa had been on the phone with Clinical Pharm, too, and between the two of us Zachary was somehow convinced to give me her Sarah's address.

I was twenty-two minutes away and fortunately traffic was on my side.

In no time I was off the freeway again and winding my way through a subdivision.

She had a garage, so I couldn't see if her car was there or not. I had to assume that it was.

I drove past her driveway and parked on the street.

Grandpa had someone who knew someone at one of the fire stations, so he assured me they were on their way.

I should wait for them.

That would be the smart thing to do.

But not smart if Sarah was in danger.

I walked right up to the front door and rang the doorbell.

There was no noise coming from inside the house. No sounds of life.

I hit the doorbell again.

Then I saw the firetruck turning the corner coming this way. Its lights were flashing, but the sirens were off.

Since Sarah's condo was on the corner, I took off around to the back door.

The gate was unlocked, so I stepped inside and went to the window. The blinds were closed. Well that didn't help.

Right about then, the police cars stopped in front of the house, sirens blaring.

I stood aside as the back door opened.

A young, clean-cut professional looking man stepped through the door, pulling Sarah with him. Her left eye was closed and her lip was busted.

My blood boiling, I took two steps forward and punched him right in the face.

He stumbled and Sarah stepped back, sinking against the wooden fence.

I grabbed him with my left hand and smacked him again with my right.

He fell down to the ground and I was on him. I slammed my fist into his nose, sending blood everywhere. I lifted my hand to hit him again.

"Luke," Sarah said, her voice reaching me through my haze of rage. "Luke. Stop."

The man appeared unconscious. She was right. He'd had enough.

As I stood up and stepped back, a fireman came through the back door followed by a policeman.

They took one look at Sarah and called for an ambulance.

"I'm okay," she insisted, going into my arms.

She was trembling all over. Shaking so badly I imagined I could hear her teeth chattering.

Billionaire's Unexpected Landing   243

What happened next was a blur.

They led us back inside her condo where we sat side by side on her sofa.

Someone put a blanket around her and I held her close.

"I need to take your statement," the policeman said. "but if you want to get cleaned up, I can take some pictures."

"Pictures?" Sarah asked.

"Of your injuries, ma'am," he said.

Sarah looked at me questioningly.

I gently swept a strand of hair off her forehead. "You've got a busted lip, love, and you're going to have a black eye."

She touched her fingers to her lips and gasped as they came back bloody.

"Okay," she said, nodding to the policeman.

When I slid mere inches away from her so he could take the pictures, she looked at me, her eyes wide. "I'm right here. Don't worry." I put my hand over hers.

And I would be right next to her for as long as she needed me.

77

SARAH

I sat on the little bench at my vanity in my upstairs bathroom and winced as Luke gently cleaned my swollen lip.

"You seem to know what you're doing," I said.

"With three brothers, I better. We found that it took a whole lot longer to clean each other up than to punch on each other."

I almost smiled, but it hurt too much. "You had to clean each other up?"

"My mother insisted. It was her rule. You pound on each other, you clean each other up. Then you sit together and have lunch or dinner or whatever the next meal was." He rinsed out the cloth and started on my eye.

"It made you really close, didn't it?" she asked.

"You bet."

When he stopped, I opened my eyes and looked into his intense blue eyes.

"I've never been hit before," I said, carefully licking my swollen bottom lip.

"And you never will again," Luke said, with an emphasis telling me he meant it.

I smiled. It hurt, but I smiled, even if was a bit one-sided.

"Thank you," I said, barely able to speak over the lump in my throat.

He picked up a brush and carefully brushed my hair. "Does your head hurt?" he asked.

"A little bit," I said. "My ears are ringing."

"That should go away." He set the brush down and studied me again. "The police are waiting downstairs to talk to you."

"I know," I said.

I had about a hundred thousand questions, but they could wait.

The first one was, of course, how did he find me?

Luke pulled my hair back. "Do you want a clean shirt?"

I nodded. "Okay."

After he stepped away to get me a shirt, I looked in the mirror. I looked like hell. I had never been in a fight or even any kind of accident to end up looking battered like this. I lifted the sleeve of my t-shirt and looked at my arm. Already I could see bruises. Jeremy had grabbed me so many times, there was no definitive handprint. Just a smattering of bruises.

He came back with a clean, white button-down shirt. One of my favorites. "Is this okay?" he asked.

"Perfect."

"Want me to help you?" he asked.

I rolled my eyes at him.

"Can't blame a guy for trying," he said, and stepped out of the bathroom. "I'll be right outside the door."

I pulled the t-shirt off over my head and put on the clean shirt, taking my time buttoning it. The police could wait. I didn't even want to think about what kind of damage they had done to my condo. Whatever might need to be cleaned up and repaired. Besides, that really didn't matter anymore.

"Okay," I said, my voice low, wondering if Luke would hear me.

He immediately opened the door and stepped inside. "You look good," he said.

I shook my head. "I look like hell."

He gently took my hand. "You look beautiful to me."

"Are you saying you like a woman with bruises on her face?" I was trying to be funny, but saying it out loud made my eyes tear up.

He pulled me to my feet and wrapped his arms around me.

"It will never happen again," he said. "You're safe now."

And I believed him. I believed him so much it hurt more than the busted lip, but in a good kind of way.

78

LUKE

Later that evening

Everything was done. Police reports. The lock on the front door was repaired.

Jeremy was in jail.

It was baffling to me that a psychiatrist could get so twisted up in the head that he thought he could force Sarah into a relationship with him.

One where he dragged her around her by the arm and hit her in the face.

I would talk to Grandma about him later. And Aunt Madison, too. If Sarah said it was ok.

We sat on the sofa, The Weather Channel playing on the television in the background. I was trying to keep things as normal as I could. I remember Uncle Jackson telling me about how important that was after Aunt Brianna had a stalker.

I don't know why he told me that. It had come up at one of our Worthington family gatherings. He and I had been sitting alone and I'd notice how he was watching Brianna.

"Do you want to go out for dinner?" I asked.

She shook her head. Her face was already turning all sorts of different colors.

"I'd rather just have something delivered," she said.

"Okay," I said. I understood. She was going to have to go out in public at some point, but not today.

"I don't want to be alone," she said, turning to me.

"You're not alone," I said.

"Yeah. No. I mean tonight."

"I'm not leaving you." I pulled her close to me.

And God help me if I didn't mean it.

Mostly to distract myself, I pulled out my phone and opened up my delivery app. "What are you hungry for?"

She thought for about half a minute. "Pizza."

I laughed, but she was serious.

So after I ordered the pizza, I found a bottle of wine in her kitchen wine rack, opened it, and filled two glasses.

I held up my glass for a toast. "To happy endings."

She tipped her glass to mine.

"How do you think he got that box to my door?" she asked.

"I meant to tell you," I said. Actually I was going to wait until she wanted to talk about it, but I was going to tell her. "The police said he used a drone."

She sat up straighter. "A drone?"

"Yeah." I shrugged. I refused to be impressed by anything Jeremy did.

"That means he was nearby." She put her fingertips against her forehead. "He must have followed me home this morning. That's how he knew where to find me."

She looked at me, searching my eyes. "He followed me out of town, didn't he?"

"He had to have," I said. "Your address is locked down like Fort Knox."

Sitting back again, she took another sip of the wine.

"You and I need to talk. You know that, right?"

We need to talk. Four words no man ever wanted to hear. My stomach turned over and I realized I had not eaten all day.

"Can we eat first?" I asked.

Whatever it was, I did not want to have a serious discuss on an empty stomach.

In fact... I set my wine glass aside.

I needed to be alert. The wine was meant to relax Sarah. And even though Jeremy was in jail, I still felt like I needed to be alert.

And, I thought, I probably always would from now on. I suddenly understood why Uncle Jackson had been looking Aunt Brianna the way he had that day.

Sarah Lawrence had my heart.

If I did nothing else in my life, I would protect and care for her.

79

SARAH

*A*fter we finished eating, I lay on my sofa with my head in Luke's lap. His fingers idly running through my hair.

There was a movie on, a romance I'd seen a hundred times, but I wasn't watching it. Not really. It was just there, giving off the only light in the room. I closed my eyes, letting the movie fade into the background.

I hadn't expected to feel this relaxed tonight. Not here in my condo. Not after all that had happened.

But Luke had that effect on me. He calmed me. I could trust him.

I knew that as long as I was with him, nothing bad would happen to me.

Even though I still had a busted lip and a black eye, I was going to be okay. I might move out of this condo, but I was going to be okay.

"Have you thought about what you're going to do about work?"

"What do you mean?" I asked, turning my head just enough that I could almost see him in the dim light.

"Since you didn't get the job in Houston, are you going to stay in your current job or are you going to do something else?"

I turned back, looking in the general direction of the television. He just jumped right in with the hard questions. "I don't know what else I would do if I didn't go back to my job," I said, but I had been letting that very question simmer in the back of my mind.

"You know a lot about psychotropic medications," he said. "You could do something with that."

"What?"

"My grandmother—the one who was a drug rep—went back to graduate school. Became a psychologist."

"I thought about doing that," I said. Maybe a little. Not seriously. I was always too busy. Traveling was a job in itself. But his grandmother wasn't the only one of us who had used the drug rep gig as a jumping off point to graduate school.

"Something to think about," Luke said, absently running a finger along the back of my ear.

I needed to talk to Luke about the messages I'd seen on his phone. Telling him I read his messages, even accidentally, might change the way he thought about me. I hoped it didn't, but we couldn't not talk about it.

"I didn't mean to see the messages on your phone," I blurted. I just wanted to get the conversation over with.

His fingers stilled and I held my breath. *Please don't let this be the end of us.* I'd tried to imagine how I would have reacted if he had looked at my messages. I think I wouldn't have worried too much about it, but I didn't have anything to hide.

"The ones about Zoe," he said, his fingers moving again.

"Yes." I slowly let out my breath. He sounded quite calm and unconcerned.

"I haven't spoken to Father about it. To clarify why he sent me that. But don't worry. I will. And you don't have to worry about her." He waited a beat. "If she is pregnant, it's not mine. I've never gone near her."

I didn't answer right away. I didn't know what to say. None of this thing with his family and Zoe was any of my business. He didn't owe me any kind of explanation.

"Sarah," he said. "My family is close-knit and I work for our family company, but they don't run me. Not like that."

"You don't have to explain," I said.

"But I want to," he said. "I need you to know." He nudged me into a sitting position, took my hand, and looked into my eyes.

"My Father is insane if he thinks I'm going to marry Zoe—anyone—for some kind of business deal."

"It is kind of... unusual." Odd. Very odd.

"Come back to Houston with me," he said. "Let's start over. I want to court you properly."

A bubble of laughter escaped my lips. "Court me?"

He shrugged sheepishly. "I can't wait for you to meet my grandmother."

"Dr. Savannah Worthington?" I asked.

"Yes." I could see the pride in his expression. "And my grandfather, Noah. You're going to love them. We'll just avoid my father."

I laughed again. "We can't avoid your father."

He grinned and I realized I had not told him no.

"I have a lot of things I need to think about," I said. "To do."

"We could go write your letter of resignation," he said, with a wink.

My thoughts froze for a split second. It took me a minute for my brain to process that. This was not a psycho. This was Luke. And he was not going to force me to do anything.

There was one thing I could tell already, though. Life with Luke Worthington was never going to be boring.

80

LUKE

Two Weeks Later

*I*t was a beautiful day for flying. Clear skies with a bank of white puffy clouds on the horizon. The sun behind us.

The Houston runway was merely minutes away.

I prepared for landing.

Sarah sat next to me in the copilot's seat, looking adorable wearing a headset. On the flight from L.A. to Houston, she'd alternated between watching everything I did to looking out the window.

It had been a busy two weeks. The two of us had been attached at the hip, working side by side.

I'd gone with her to speak to Zachary. He'd turned pale at the sight of her face and instantly offered her time off from work.

It had only taken a brief conversation from there for that time off from work to become her two weeks notice.

He admitted that he had expected her to get the job in

Houston, so even though she didn't get it, he had a contingency plan already in place.

We had packed up her condo. I'd never known a woman, other than my Aunt Brianna—a self-proclaimed minimalist—to have so few belongings. But even Aunt Brianna would have had a lot of furniture to move. Sarah wasn't taking hers. She was selling her condo furnished.

Everything had just fallen into place. The packing. Getting the condo listed for sale.

Once again, I had used my status as the boss's son to take the time off I needed.

She and I had talked about just about everything, except maybe our future together.

I knew what I wanted, but I wasn't going to rush her.

I wanted to give her time to put her experience with psycho Jeremy behind her.

After a perfect landing, I taxied over to the Skye Travels terminal and went through my post-flight checklist.

It was good to be home. And it felt surreal that Sarah had actual agreed to uproot her life to come with me.

We'd made a quick trip up to her country home to grab a few things, including the box of letters written between Nathaniel and Rebecca.

I'd looked it up for her and discovered that the two of them had indeed gotten married on Nathaniel's two-day furlough. Their first child had come along nine months later.

I'd already asked Sarah to marry me, but I'd been using Nathaniel's words and, of course, she had not answered. I was going propose for real. To do it right. But I had to figure out the timing.

I took off my headset, took off my sunshades, and turned to Sarah.

"Welcome home," I said.

Billionaire's Unexpected Landing   255

She smiled. Her lip was healed and her bruises were barely visible, even without makeup.

"Don't be nervous," I said. "My family is going to love you."

"I'm not," she said. "I'm with you."

I grinned and leaned over to press a kiss lightly against her lips.

Sometimes the most random, unexpected things in life were the most important.

Just a last minute passenger pick up at the end of an otherwise normal day.

EPILOGUE

I stood at the window looking out over the city of Houston from the twenty-ninth floor of Luke's condo. Our condo. A tower in the sky. A very secure tower in the sky. No one could come up the elevator without a fob and even then, the elevator person had to recognize them.

It was a beautiful clear day, rays from the midday sun coming in through the window. White puffy clouds off to the southeast.

The University of Houston was down there somewhere. I'd spent some time browsing their website, getting acquainted with their psychology graduate department.

Luke would be home any time now and we would head over to his grandparent's house for Saturday dinner.

Unless there was a flight delay, Luke was reliably punctual.

Two minutes later, I heard the elevator door slide open.

"Honey," he said. "I'm home."

I met him in the living room.

"I brought you something," he said.

"A surprise?"

"Of course."

Billionaire's Unexpected Landing   257

I'd never liked surprises much, but Luke's surprises were always good and I was adapting.

He pulled a bouquet of purple tulips from behind his back.

He paid attention to everything, including quickly learning that purple was my favorite color.

Although he hadn't said it, I knew he was afraid to give me roses. He'd been slowly giving me other flowers, making sure I was okay with it.

But I felt nothing but joy as I took the flowers from him. I refused to let what happened with Jeremy color the rest of my life.

He pulled me into a hug.

"I have something to show you, too," I said.

"What is it?" he asked.

Taking his hand, I led him toward the room we were using as our study.

I picked up a letter and, trying to keep a blank expression, handed it to him.

"What's this?" he asked.

I bit my lip and just lifted a brow.

He carefully took the paper out of the envelope and began reading.

Then he grabbed me up, my feet leaving the floor, and twirled me around.

"You did it," he said, as I giggled. "You got in."

I'd been sitting on it all day, dying to tell someone, but wanting to tell Luke in person.

"I'm so proud of you." He set me on my feet and looked into my eyes. "You're doing this for you, right?" he asked. "Not because I encouraged it?"

"No. Yes," I said. "I'm really, really excited about it. But—"

"But?" He looked at me sideways.

"What am I going to do for two months waiting on classes to start?"

"I have some ideas about that," he said.

"Like what?"

"We could always use the time to do some planning."

"And what are we planning?" I asked. He'd already very smoothly gotten me moved in with him after putting my own condo up for sale.

"Well," he said. "I have still some courting to do," he said, kissing me lightly on the cheek.

"Courting?"

"And," he said, kissing me on the lips. "I have a two-day furlough coming up."

Keep Reading for a preview of
BILLIONAIRE'S ACCIDENTAL GIRLFRIEND ...

BILLIONAIRE'S ACCIDENTAL GIRLFRIEND PREVIEW

Chapter 1
Zoe Madris

I'm one of those girls that guys like hanging out with.

Balancing carefully on my stiletto heels, I stepped onto the escalator heading down to the hotel lobby. I wore a mid-thigh length dress that limited the length of my steps.

As a result, I have lots of friends—all guys. I'd had a girlfriend once, but she and I had nothing to talk about, so that was the end of that.

Maybe it was because I work in a man's world. As an architect, I sometimes went all day without talking to anyone other than men, especially on a construction site.

The large wall of windows might have provided a nice view, except for the incessant rain. It was the third day I'd been in Seattle and it had rained every single day. Dark and dreary. So different from the sunny skies of Houston I was used to. Today, in fact, it was one hundred three degrees in Houston.

It was a wonder any buildings ever got built in weather like this. And they said it was like this all year long.

But we were leaving out tomorrow. Three other guys and I had been hired to fly up here as consultants on the design of a new branch of my grandfather's pharmacy distribution center.

I stepped off the escalator into the lobby and headed to the bar where we were meeting. It was our last night here, so we were allowed to blow off some steam.

Maybe that was why I had chosen to wear my little red dress. It hugged my body like a glove, showing off all my accents. And on top of that, it was sequined. A solid red sequined dress. Not the kind of dress a girl usually wore when hanging out with the guys.

But, I was convinced, that was one of the things they liked about me.

I kept my men in the friend zone. But I knew that any one of them with just the crook of my finger would be more than willing to be my boyfriend.

My heels clicked as I walked across the lobby.

There was no one else around, oddly enough. But this was a convention hotel and there was no convention going on.

Music spilled out as I neared the bar. Eighties music. My favorite.

As I stepped into the bar, I slid my cell phone into my handbag.

I spotted my friends, over at a table toward the right and headed that way. There were only half a dozen other people around.

Beau held up a hand and Charlie held up a glass with his right hand. His left hand held his phone glued to his ear. How was he even hearing with the loud music?

Billionaire's Unexpected Landing 261

"Where's Trent?" I asked, sliding into the circular booth.

"Talking with Dylan." Beau slid closer to me, but not touching.

"Oh." I quickly scanned the room, but Dylan wasn't anywhere in sight.

Dylan Worthington was our designated pilot. Straight from Skye Travels.

There was something about the way he smiled at me with a little sideways grin. And the way I caught him gazing at me something like he was window shopping.

He was not my type. First of all, and most importantly, I knew for a fact that he had girlfriends all over the country.

I knew because I had flown with him from here, Seattle, to Savannah, to Phoenix, to name just three cities.

And in every one of those cities, he had a different girlfriend. Girlfriends that lived there.

That disqualified him from being any kind of friend.

My guy friends either had no girlfriends or one girlfriend.

I could not tolerate players.

The funny thing about that was that a lot of people mistakenly thought I was a player. Far from it. I didn't even have a boyfriend right now.

In any port.

"What's he talking to Dylan about?" I asked.

"He didn't say," Beau motioned for a server. "Where have you been?"

"I fell asleep," I said with a shrug.

The server came over and Beau ordered my martini, extra olives. He didn't even have to ask me what I wanted. I always ordered the same thing. One drink. That's all I ever drank.

The music changed to something romantic and a couple of older people got up and started dancing.

"Why do they do that?" Beau asked, leaning close.

"Do what?" I knew what he meant.

"Why do they dance?"

"I don't know," I said. And right now I had no care.

Dylan Worthington was coming through the door with Trent.

Dylan was one of those men who exuded sexiness.

I sat frozen. Fight or flight.

I could barely think when Dylan was around, much less hold a conversation.

Trent was leading him straight over to our booth.

There wasn't room at this booth for five. There was barely room for four.

I slid out of the booth. Right now flight was winning the battle.

"Where are you going?" Charlie asked, covering his phone. "I need to talk to you."

"We can talk later."

Trent and Dylan were standing at our booth now.

"Hey," Trent said, sliding in, knowing I couldn't stand being trapped in the middle. I always sat on the outside of the booth.

"Hey," I said, keeping my gaze on him so I didn't have to look at Dylan.

Dylan didn't seemed to have even noticed I was there. He was leaning over talking to Charlie who had finally put his cell phone away.

The server showed up with my drink and set it carefully on the table.

Dylan never hang out with us on these trips. He always had a girlfriend to go to.

I was overreacting. He would not be here long.

So I sat down and took a sip of my drink. Not bad.

"Where were you?" Trent asked.

"I took a nap," I said, cutting my eyes in his direction. "What were you doing?"

Billionaire's Unexpected Landing 263

"Talking to Dylan," he said with a little shrug. Like it was nothing to be talking to

Dylan Worthington.

Dylan was older than we were. About five years older. And his grandfather owned Skye Travels, the largest private airline company in the country.

"About what?" I asked, then kicked myself. I had no reason to have a care about what Dylan and Trent were talking about.

"Airplanes," Trent said.

"Since when do you care about airplanes?"

"When have I not?" Trent asked.

I felt Dylan's gaze sweep in my direction and once again I had that fight or flight reaction.

I would not run away.

"Sit down," I heard Charlie say.

Out of all my friends, Charlie knew how I felt about Dylan. But Charlie being Charlie, he had already had more alcohol than he needed.

"Want a drink?" Beau asked, always the one to take charge of the drinks.

"Can't," Dylan said.

Then Dylan did the unthinkable. He sat down next to me.

I automatically scooted left, but Trent wasn't budging.

As Dylan sat down, his thigh brushed against mine. I jerked away as though I had been burned, but Dylan didn't even seem to notice.

"Bottle to throttle," he said, completing his answer to Beau's question.

"Well," Charlie said. "I'll have another one."

I pushed my drink across the table toward Charlie. "Take mine," I said.

I had lost my taste for it and I was plotting a way out of here. Not having a drink was a good start.

Charlie pushed it back. "You need it."

"I'm going up to bed," I said and all four sets of eyes stared blankly at me.

"You just got up from a nap," Beau said.

"Just drink your drink. You'll feel better," Charlie said.

I made an eyeroll that encompassed both of them.

"Don't go," Trent said. "Don't leave me here with these idiots."

"You can go, too," I said, pulling my martini back in front of me and taking a sip.

"If that's an invitation," he said. "Let's go."

"You wish."

"Dylan. Where's your girlfriend?" Beau asked, changing the direction of the conversation and voicing the question that everyone wanted to know.

Now all eyes, including mine, were on Dylan.

Dylan waved off the question. "The flu or something," he said.

No backup girl? But I kept my snarky response to myself.

Dylan was not my business.

There was one problem, though. I had never been this close to him. And he smelled as good as he looked. I worked around men all day, but Dylan smelled like a pine forest and vanilla mixed with leather. And something that reminded me of… jet fuel.

Good God, he was sexy.

And he was smiling at me with that sideways grin and looked like a cat about to pounce on its prey.

I was imagining it, that was all.

I was not Dylan's type any more than he was mine.

Chapter 2
Dylan Worthington

Billionaire's Unexpected Landing

Zoe Madris was every man's wet dream come to life and I'd happily call any man a liar who said otherwise.

But she was not for me. She had plenty of boyfriends. I don't think she actually slept with them. I would know if she did. She was one of those girls who kept a bevy of men around her. It baffled me how half a dozen men were content to hang out with the one girl they all wanted.

I suppose it was like playing some kind of game. They had to stay to play.

One day, they all hoped, she would pick one of them.

I didn't like to share my women, at least not when I was with them. I liked women who weren't looking for any kind of commitment.

My women knew I would call them when I was in town. No strings. No commitment.

It was the best kind of freedom a man could have.

But right now Zoe was sitting next to me. So close that my thigh could rest against hers if I so much as shifted an inch. I experimented with it, but both times, she moved away.

She was wearing a tight red sequined dress that showed off all her perfectly formed curves. She smelled good, too.

The thing about Zoe, besides her good looks and her aloofness, was her voice.

She had a slightly husky voice that was sexy as hell.

Husky with a little southern lilt that a man could spend all day listening to.

I summed up her popularity with the men into those three things. Her beauty, her voice, and the way she didn't seem to give a damn whether a man liked her or not.

But as she slid an olive off the toothpick, wrapping those gorgeous lips around it, I saw her fingers tremble. Just a little and I doubt anyone else noticed.

Between my grandmother and two of my aunts, I grew up

around psychologists. Just listening to them talk, I'd learned enough about people to know when they were feeling nervous. Or maybe I was just more attentive to detail than most men. It was probably in my genes.

Either way, I could see that Zoe Madris was nervous right now. Since I was the only thing different, I figured I was causing it.

And me being me, I liked a challenge.

I stretched out and made myself comfortable. I decided to change the conversation away from her long enough for her to relax.

"Trent," I said, picking up our earlier conversation. "I'm happy to take you up sometime. Show you around a cockpit."

"Cool," Trent said.

I pulled out my phone. "Type your number in here."

Trent did as asked, then slid my phone back.

I leaned toward Zoe as I picked it up.

This time she didn't pull away.

Well, that was interesting. But, then, she was practically sitting in Trent's lap to keep from touching me.

Not the usual response I got from women.

When the server came by with another drink for Charlie, I ordered a ginger ale.

This was actually a more entertaining evening than I had planned. Shelly, bless her heart, was a sure thing. I know she wanted more than just a casual relationship, so it was about time for me to cut her free.

"Do you have to file a fight plan for that? Or can you just fly around?" Trent asked.

"Depends on where you are and what type aircraft you're flying," I said.

"When you're flying IFR," Zoe said.

We all turned and looked at her.

She shrugged. "If the airport has a tower, you have to get

Billionaire's Unexpected Landing   **267**

clearance to taxi and takeoff, but as long as you're flying VFR, you don't have to."

When no one said anything, she added. "It's still a good idea to do so though in case you crash."

"How do you know that?" Trent asked.

"She's smarter than the average bear," Charlie said.

She just shrugged.

I think I just might be in love.

I grinned as the server dropped off my drink.

"I'll have another," Charlie said.

We all knew Charlie did not need another drink, but none of us said anything. Not even Zoe.

She was the first woman I'd ever met who didn't chastise a man for drinking too much AND she knew flight language.

As much as I hated to admit it, I was starting to understand her allure.

And damn it. That pissed me off.

I did not want to be another of Zoe's men.

"We can bring Zoe flying with us," Trent said.

Zoe shot him a go to hell look.

He just grinned.

"Absolutely," I said.

"I wanna go, too," Charlie said.

"Sure thing, buddy." It was better to just agree than to tell him that he was one too many.

So was Trent, but I'd figure something out about that.

"The only thing that sucks," Charlie said. "Is you can't drink."

"It's not so bad," I said.

Sometimes it was actually a good excuse. Sometimes a man just wanted to keep his wits about him.

Zoe ate another olive off her toothpick and to my chagrin, I was one of four men who watched, mesmerized.

Looked like she wasn't drinking either.

She was different than I'd expected.

There was something about Zoe.

Something I did not understand.

But whatever it was, I was determined to figure it out.

As we talked for a few more minutes, Zoe sat quietly, nibbling on her olives. She still wasn't relaxed enough for her leg or her arm to touch mine, but her hands weren't trembling anymore. That was a good sign.

I was making progress on that front.

And yet I was getting more baffled about my own reaction. To her.

Not to be outdone, I turned and looked right at her.

She looked up at me and I forgot whatever it was I had on my mind.

She had the most mesmerizing green eyes. Even in the dim light of the bar, I could see the depth in those eyes.

I could see how they would suck a man in deep and not let him go. Not me, though.

Still. My pants were feeling a bit tight around the crotch.

She looked away and I felt like I'd stepped out of the sunshine.

Good God.

What the hell was wrong with me?

Charlie started making a ruckus across the table.

"What wrong with you, Charlie," Beau asked.

"Damn it," Charlie answered, digging in his pockets.

Beau put a hand on his arm. "What are you doing?"

Charlie looked around at us. "Cut it out," he said.

"Cut what out?" Trent asked.

"Who took my key?"

Beau looked over at Zoe. "He's had too much."

Zoe shrugged. "He's your roommate."

"We need to get him to bed."

Billionaire's Unexpected Landing   269

"Give it back," Charlie said. "Who's got my key?"

Zoe, Beau, and Trent all three took out their room keys and laid them on the table. It looked they had done this before.

Charlie looked at me. "You," he said. "You took my key."

I tried not to laugh. "Why would I—?"

"He won't stop 'til you show him your key," Beau said.

With a little shake of my head, I pulled out my money clip and slid out my room key. Set it on the table in front of me along with everyone else.

"He doesn't have it," Zoe said.

Beau motioned to the server and ordered five glasses of water.

Charlie stood up on wobbly legs, digging in his pockets.

The server was back and began setting glasses of water on the table.

Charlie looked surprised when he pulled a room key out of his back pocket.

"Damn," he said and flopping back down, knocking over one of the glasses of water.

The server was fast. I had to give her that.

She whipped out a towel and began sopping up the water before it got all of us wet.

They had their hands full with Charlie and I wanted nothing to do with it.

"It's been real," I said. "See you all in the morning at nine a.m."

Since I had my money clip out, I slapped a hundred down and grabbed up my room key.

Beau and Trent said "See 'ya."

Charlie didn't seem to even notice and Zoe didn't say anything.

My phone vibrated just as I neared the escalator.

SHELLY: *Hey baby. I have a surprise for you.*

Too late for a surprise. I did, however, need to make a phone call home, so I made a detour and stepped outside for some fresh air.

Keep Reading BILLIONAIRE'S ACCIDENTAL GIRLFRIEND...